THE STRENGTH OF TIME

by   Shirley Mason

ALSO BY SHIRLEY MASON

The CAV NEUMONT series:
    The Strength of Water (1)
    The Strength of Love   (3)
    The Strength of Mercy (4)
Five Couples
Murder for Short (stories)
Send Help   (stories)

Disclaimer

All places are fictitious except for Chipping Campden and London, which are real places, and all events and people are the product of the author's imagination, except for the ghost, Lady Joan, and her name has been changed to protect the innocent.

Publisher: CREATESPACE
Copyright © Shirley Mason (2015)

ISBN 978-0-578-70437-1 (Paperback)

First Published 2015. Austin Macauley Publishers Ltd.
The right of Shirley Mason Larsen to be identified as author of this work has been asserted by her in accordance with section 77 and 78 of the UL Copyright, Designs and Patents Act 1988.

For Bertel, Sr.

THE STRENGTH OF TIME

by Shirley Mason

PART ONE

I

Lady Mardling Must Adjust

The peace that surpasses all understanding flowed in concentric circles around Cav Neumont Manor and its surrounding lands. Emma Chapman and Lord Simon Appleby Haversham, 5th Earl of Cav Neumont, walked about and talked about things odd and ordinary. Sometimes Lord Haversham's cat, Schrödinger, followed at a respectful distance, so as not to eavesdrop. And when Emma and his lordship were not outside looking at the lane of lilac trees, they were having tea, or dinner with John Britely, his lordship's estate manager and friend, and on occasion were joined by neighbors Lady Mardling and Lady Southway. Those dear, but sometimes acerbic, women had lately, but reluctantly, accepted the fact of Emma's staying at the manor on a rather full-time basis. Perhaps not permanently, they hoped. They kept that hope to themselves.

Prior to Ms. Chapman's arrival, Lady Mardling thought her path clear to the desirable and available Lord Haversham, and as well, Lady Southway wasn't much content to be in second place, but hanging on the edge was rather better than dropping off altogether. Although unknown and unproven, and certainly never discussed except behind tightly shut doors, Lord Haversham's income was rumored to be second only to the royal treasury, and with such he was able to fill his days maintaining the ancient and vast manor. He and his ancestors had loved and maintained the manor, orchards, and grounds now for five generations. In addition, he put in a few days each month in London advising the Minister of the Interior, which duty gave him just enough look at England's commerce, politics, and traffic as he could bear away from his beloved county seat.

Emma had first met Lord Haversham the previous fall when she came to his village for a hiking tour. After a distracting social detour when she was tricked by Lord Haversham's grounds man, Troy, into thinking that *he, Troy,* was the lord of the manor, and after surviving the cunning of his lordship's former wife, Lady Claire, who had sent Emma packing with the assurance that she, Lady Claire, had come back to stay—Emma had returned to the manor, having recently arrived again from the States.

She and Lord Haversham (Simon to his close friends and family) had arrived at the truth—that they had learned to care deeply for each other. Both were happily relieved that they had cleared up the misunderstanding Lady Claire had maliciously caused, and they felt that any minute away from each other's presence was a waste of time. Their temperaments melded perfectly like chocolate and sugar.

Lord Haversham wanted to keep Emma at the manor for as long as she would stay. His intentions were most honorable—he would win her if he could, and he understood that she was someone special, not to be won easily. He had first been captivated by the way her dark tresses bounced, and then he found that he admired her firm, lithe frame—there was a grace about the way she moved—and his heart seemed to skip in a happy manner when her eyes sought his. Without sensing all that, she was drawn to his way of pulling back his mouth into that soft smile that always seemed to point her to his silver sideburns. And she found herself listening carefully to his voice—that mysterious appeal. Hard to explain.

This evening the present company included Emma, Lady Mardling, Lady Southway, and John Britely, and while they waited for Brooks, Lord Haversham's butler, to announce dinner, his lordship's preference was palpable throughout the room; he and Emma seemed to share every glance and thought; he took Emma's hand at every opportunity.

Schrödinger showed his preference also, by rubbing against Emma's shoe, and—other than a liking as well for Lord Haversham's shoe and his adopted son, Peter's, shoe, and those of the staff—Schrödinger was not drawn to others. An unsettling state of affairs for the Ladies Mardling and Southway, who, while pretending pleasure, could only look on with displeasure. They had come to know the significance of Schrödinger's gestures.

And then there was Major, the golden Labrador, new addition to the manor. Clearly Major preferred Simon and Ms. Chapman, who, during their daily walks, had been putting the dog through training exercises followed by treats of the canine kind. Major was there to stay. Lady Mardling said to his lordship that he wasn't happy unless he could introduce another problem to the manor: this time in the form of an additional not-too-bright, four-legged pest, or pet, she meant to say.

"Major is in training," his lordship had replied. "Indeed, he makes mistakes; he's young. He'll learn and be one of the finest critters ever seen at the manor. Even Lady Joan indicated her approval."

"How you jest, Simon. How could a ghost show approval?"

"It's quite true, Agnes, I jest not. When I put Major's bed in place next to my bed, and led him to it, Lady Joan arrived and smiled down on him." This was only partly true: Lord Haversham had placed Major's bed, and had led the dog to it, but Lady Joan, unpredictable as she was, had not appeared. However, rousing Lady Mardling's sensibilities always gave his lordship a jolly good turn.

Sufficiently chastened, Lady Mardling turned to the one person more threatening than Major, that is to say, Emma. "Ms. Chapman," Lady Mardling said, "don't you have an occupation in the States?"

"Yes, Lady Mardling. However, I have freelanced for years at various positions, and can usually decide when I'll take a contract, and for how long."

3

"What can be so unimportant that you can come and go?" Lady Mardling asked.

"Well, some of my contracts have an urgent aspect and others less so. Some require a real test of my training, others less so. Sometimes, I do nothing but sit in a law library and search for statutes and precedents. Each contract is different. I prefer that. It never bores."

This sounded too pat for Lady Mardling; she looked around the drawing room for inspiration, something to suggest an idea with which she could puncture Emma's perfect setup. Her eyes lit on the butler's bell. "Do any of the law firms you work for call for you again?"

"Yes, indeed. For the last three years, I've worked for only two firms. Their legal focus varies, so I am able to work on different kinds of legal matters. You heard about the recent one in Arizona. That was a tort case of national scope."

"The one when you were arrested for murder."

"Not arrested, Lady Mardling, just asked not to leave town until they had found the culprit. I continued to work in Tucson for that contract, and, as you know, they did arrest someone for the murder."

Lady Mardling knew that story, and though no one at the manor took her seriously, especially not Lord Haversham, she twisted it now and then to put Emma in a bad light. "I see," she said. "And at this time I venture you are not in the middle of a contract." A pity, she thought.

Lord Haversham, John Britely, and Lady Southway listened to this exchange, his lordship wishing there were an easy, inoffensive way to curtail the barbs of his long-standing neighbor, Lady Mardling. He hadn't many neighbors, only she and Lady Southway and Sophia Bachman, who rented one of the manor's cottages, and dwelled there sometimes and sometimes not. And though his lordship did enjoy his fairly solitary life, he did still need his neighbors, and they were at heart, good people.

"Right. I left a colleague in Manhattan to finish two estate closings for me," Emma said. "They were simple, and she didn't mind. I finished closings for her when she took sick leave; you might say she owed me the favor. Lord Simon has been so kind to suggest that I invite her here to show appreciation, and she's eager to come over. We expect her on Friday, Brenda Evans is her name. I expect she'll be here for a week or so."

"Indeed, Simon is so liberal," Lady Mardling said, planting an admonition on Lord Haversham, "opening up the manor to strangers."

At once, Lord Haversham felt a force; it seemed dark and foreboding, and he did not know why, and did not know its origins, but in Lady Mardling's tone there was a warning that for the first time affected him deeply. He ignored her remark, but bristled as usual that he must be on a first name acquaintance with her. "Agnes," he countered finally, for the room waited for his reaction, "that is true. If she will laugh with us, she's welcome."

And for a flicker of a second, Lady Mardling suspected that she herself was the one inspiring a laugh.

Brooks announced dinner and the five people went through. Simon couldn't take all three ladies' arms, and clearly his first choice was Emma's. How vexing. Still Lady Mardling hoped Emma would have to return to the States before something serious took place—if she would only *stay* there. Lady Mardling could do nothing but wait and see. It had been a while since she had Simon to herself, and now another woman was about to arrive. Even when after Christmas, she followed Simon to Lake Como, Lady Southway was always with them. And then Simon left for home so abruptly, didn't give them notice until the day he left, which reduced the ladies to making their way home without him. Now seated at the dining table, the next most vexing thing was that Simon seated Emma at his right. As Simon's oldest acquaintance, Lady Mardling felt she should have that position, or preferably, the foot of the table, but Simon made certain, by having an enormous flower arrangement placed there, that no one took the foot.

After all were seated, Lady Mardling continued; she needed to get to the bottom of something, needed more information. "And, Ms. Chapman, you don't have to be back for another contract now?" She did not miss the look that passed between Simon and Emma.

"No, not yet," Emma said. "I have no further obligation there. Actually, I have a new one in mind, right in London. That won't start for a week or two. The law firm for which I worked in Arizona, Tortle and Gainer, has started consulting with a London firm on an international maritime case. As paralegal, I have a good bit of experience in that field, and Greg Tortle has asked whether I would take a contract with them in London. It's a convenient coincidence for me . . . I enjoyed working for Tortle."

"I see," Lady Mardling said. "Too bad, my dear, that you have to work."

"It's quite interesting, Lady Mardling, and I have sufficient time for vacation."

Lady Mardling could not summon up another barb, and the group attended to their dinner.

II

Brenda Arrives on the Train

On Friday, Brenda Evans arrived with all her finery. And although Emma had warned her that a backpack with casual clothes and a dress for dinner would suffice, Brenda arrived with two large suitcases and a smaller one for make-up. At first, as Emma and John Britely scanned the passengers who were stepping down from the train, Emma didn't recognize Brenda; the vision of the tall, slender, blonde beauty wearing a long ruffled blue skirt and wide-brimmed red hat, took its time assuring Emma that this was indeed Brenda. Even in Manhattan, Emma had not seen her dressed so smartly.

"Simon! I'm so thrilled to meet you," Brenda said. "I've heard so much about you." She had bypassed Emma altogether in the rush to pump John Britely's hand.

For a second, torn between trying to apologize for being himself and not Lord Haversham, and working to free his hand, John's reply was caught in his throat.

Emma relaxed her amazement and said, "Brenda, it's so good to see you. This is Mr. Britely, Lord Haversham's estate manager. Lord Haversham won't be in until later this evening. He had business today in London."

Brenda looked from Emma to John Britely and back, her face uncomprehending. Then she recovered enough to say, "Mr. Britely, you look *so* important, I just knew you would be the lord of the manor. 'To the manor born', they say." She tittered, large teeth gaining ground.

"Indeed," he said. "Fortunately, I am not," and he allowed a flicker of a smile.

Brenda turned back to Emma. "Hello, Emma."

Emma managed to mummer something not quite audible.

"This way, Miss Evans," John said, and he and Emma picked up the three suitcases that the porter had set beside them, and followed Brenda, skirt swishing ahead of them, off the platform. "I'll bring the car round," John said. Otherwise, he thought, in those fragile high heels, Miss Evans would never make it to the car.

At the manor, Emma took Brenda to her room, helped her settle in, explained where her own room was down another hall, and showed her the bell cord with which she could call Ellie, the upstairs maid. "When you are ready, Ellie will bring up a tray of supper for you and will help with anything else you might need."

"But am I not to meet Lord Haversham tonight?" Brenda asked.

"No. It's too late. You'll meet him in the morning. Ellie will let you know when and will show you the way to the morning room where we usually meet for breakfast."

THE NEXT MORNING Ellie knocked at Brenda's door to ask whether she wanted a tray in her room, and if not, to take her down. That settled, when Brenda was ready, Ellie led her down to breakfast where Emma, Lord Haversham, and John Britely were assembled around the sparkling table. Brooks, just coming in with a pot of coffee, directed Brenda to serve herself from the array of breakfast foods spread across the sideboard. He then poured Brenda's coffee, and pulled out a chair for her to the left of his lordship, next to John.

Lord Haversham and John Britely stood and greeted her with a smile. And after the proper introductions had taken place, he said, "Miss Evans, welcome to Cav Neumont Manor. Even the sun seems to have come out to welcome you."

"Did you have a restful night?" John asked.

Brenda appeared not to notice John as she turned to Lord Haversham. "Simon. Is it alright if I call you Simon? Please call me Brenda; I feel I know you already. Emma talks about you all the time."

This was hardly true; Emma had not worked with Brenda at the Free Title Company in New York for more than six weeks, and other than a few lunches, had had no personal contact with her. And anyway, Emma wasn't one to discuss her personal life; nor during the work day was there time for small talk. Emma, her face arranged into a question, stared at Brenda. "Why, Brenda . . . that could give the wrong impression."

Lord Haversham's reply was garbled, muffled.

Brenda didn't appear to hear it, instead ignored Emma and continued, "I'm dying for you to show me around this grand palace."

Lord Haversham had no wrong impression. Indeed, he felt that Miss Evans over-spoke. To his shame, he remembered his past mistake of referring to "Americans who gush", the time he misspoke within Emma's hearing and alienated her before he had even met her. Fortunately, Emma had forgiven him—more than forgiven; he had earned a corner of her heart, and was setting about seeing to it that that corner grew. And yet, now here before him was a gushing American.

"Ah. . .," his mouth was stuck open. A house tour. . . indeed. *Palace!* Perhaps he would ask Mrs. Penrose to perform the tour. She knew the *palace* better than he did; she ran the *palace*. "I'll ask our housekeeper, Mrs. Penrose, to give you a tour, Miss Evans. She knows the manor better than I do."

"But Simon, I would love to see it through your eyes."

By way of answer, as though he hadn't heard Miss Evans, he moved those eyes, along with a morsel of bacon, over to Schrödinger perched nearby on his tower. Indeed, he vowed he would find ways to avoid Miss Evans altogether if he could. He paused to consider what had brought Miss Brenda Evans here: she had called Emma from the States, and he had been privy to the call. She had called to tell Emma that the two estate closings she had finished for her, had signed off perfectly. Emma had researched the property titles, and mortgage applications, and drawn up the contracts, so that when Emma left for England, Miss Evans had only to explain the details to the principals, get signatures, collect and distribute funds. His lordship had listened to Emma thanking Miss Evans with assurances that she couldn't have made this trip had Miss Evans not been so kind to cover for her.

"My dear, Emma," he had butted in before Emma had a chance to tell him that she really didn't know Brenda well, "tell your colleague we have a room for her here at the manor. Tell her to come over, if she can get leave. She helped you and we would like to have her visit and show her about." Brenda had heard him and had accepted immediately. That's how it happened. Now, when he would have had a chance for Emma and him to be close, they seemed distant with the arrival of this new, invasive, watchful woman. Already he felt it so. Well, her visit couldn't be permanent. He had ways of casting out unwanted guests. Time in its patient wisdom would show him the way to do so.

For a few seconds no one spoke. They buttered toast, cracked eggs, and sipped coffee.

"And how is Luke?" Emma asked Brenda, hoping to change the direction of Brenda's imposing on Simon. Luke was Brenda's live-together partner back in the States. But Emma wasn't prepared for Brenda's reply.

"Oh, Luke said to give you his love. He wants you to hurry back." Brenda fixed on Emma her sweetest, strongest smile, brows up as though to say, 'See how lucky you are. You have someone.'

"Hurry back?" Emma said. "Surely he's teasing you . . . why I've hardly ever seen Luke. We merely passed documents between each other at work. I thought you and he had a commitment?" Emma hadn't asked, and Brenda hadn't said, but it was obvious that Brenda and Luke arrived and left work together those last few weeks.

Emma's question was lost on Brenda, for Brenda was concentrating on applying jam to toast, and she didn't look up. She merely said, "Hmm." Then she said, "Simon, how long have you lived here?"

Looking down at his plate as though he might find something there to repel her intrusion, he waited exactly five seconds before he said, "I was born here."

"Born here? My, that's odd. You must be the only person I know who lives in the house where he was born."

"It's not uncommon in the United Kingdom," he said.

"Really!"

"Right. We're not as mobile in the same way as Americans with your vast reaches. We tend to take employment close to home as well."

"What is your job?" Brenda asked.

The choke in Lord Haversham's throat prevented ready speech; he needed another few seconds to find a reply. He tried not to look at her as she gestured to him with the jam spoon, yet some compelling kind of amazement made him stare at her gestures. Emma began to explain, but Lord Haversham's reply found itself and he gave it.

"My *job*, as you put it, Miss Evans, is maintaining this *palace*, also as you put it. The grounds are vast and Mr. Britely, the staff, and I, work at this full-time. It does take that much work, though I know, that on the surface it appears to run itself. And, as well, I have a minor position with the Cabinet."

"The Cabinet?" Brenda said. "What's that?"

"Government, Miss Evans. Indeed, it requires that I be in London frequently."

"Oh, government. How exciting! I want to hear all about that, Simon."

John Britely closed off a laugh. Lord Haversham looked to Emma and John for help. He had stepped into more than he meant to. Nothing seemed to curb this woman's ill-formed manners. What had he introduced into his home? Emma could only look at her plate, as though peace on earth could be found there.

To recover, change the subject, keep it light, his lordship said in a mocking tone, "Our palace . . . has a ghost, Miss Evans. Her name is Lady Joan. You might run into her . . . so to speak."

"Simon! A ghost! Please protect me from her, lest I faint. And *please* call me Brenda. Stay close to me, for I don't know what I'd do if I saw her. Will she appear in my room?"

He resolved never to address her as Brenda. "No one can know where Lady Joan will appear, Miss Evans. But she's benevolent, quite a guardian of the *palace*." He stifled the urge to say, *your room is a favorite hangout of Lady Joan's, and she's unpredictable*.

"I see. Still, if she appears in my room when I'm there, you'll hear my scream. Can't I move to a room near yours? I'd feel so much safer," she said, her face screwing itself into a plea.

"You'll have adequate company in your hall," he said.

"I'm nearby and also Peter," John Britely said, "when he's down from college. And Lady Joan has never done harm. Scary to see though. As well, she sometimes makes scary moans." Not likely, he thought, Lady Joan has always been most pleasant; but a bit of embellishment wouldn't hurt. He understood the fix his lordship felt them to be in with this American visitor.

Brenda looked skeptical.

It occurred to Lord Haversham that this was a new service Lady Joan could perform for the so-called *palace*: scare off unwanted guests.

"And that brings up a question, Simon."

Ah, so he feared.

"As my room is far away and down a different hall from Emma's . . . quite far away . . . why are the bedrooms distributed so? I felt so alone last night."

His lordship had no desire to give her an explanation; no desire to give her an explanation for anything at all. Yet everyone was looking to him for his answer. He might just get it over with. "The front-facing wing of the manor was laid out above stairs so that the principal rooms . . . two-bedroom suites . . . capture the morning sun, and have a view over the east terrace, the drive, and lilac trees. A small study, as well, flows along that side. Then down your corridor, suites are designed for a view across the valley to cliffs and to let in a bit of the afternoon sun. When there is sun, that is. You're in good company on the same hall as Mr. Britely." His lordship wanted to underplay the good company part, wanted to play to Brenda's unease, wanted to play to keeping her visit short. Even so, he was ever the good host.

"Emma said her room is called 'Solar.' Why is that?" Emma had already explained the designation, but Brenda wanted to hear

Simon's explanation; to hear him speak about anything. Draw him in.

"Solar, a special room indeed, is named after an ancient and famous room," he said. "Emma . . ." he washed over her a look that said, *thank goodness you are who you are*, "if you like, you can take the golf cart to show Miss Evans the village shops. Or, if you prefer, I'll have Brooks ask Hadley to drive you there. You might even enjoy the walk . . . it's but four miles. I often walk it."

"Four miles!" Brenda said. "I don't think so."

"Brenda, you walk that every day in Manhattan, don't you?" Emma said.

"Oh, no. I take a cab or the subway."

The unexpected tune jangling through the room caused forks to stop mid-air, and at least one to clatter in astonishment as heads turned to question the loud interruption.

"Oh," Brenda said, and she dug in her pocket to retrieve her mobile phone. She looked at its face to see who was calling, then said. "Hello, you tiger! You wouldn't believe where I am right now . . . having breakfast with Lord Haversham at the grandest table you could imagine. Butler and all! Wish you could see it. You could make a bowling alley out of this table." While the others stared at her with disbelief, she continued to prattle on to the caller, interjecting numerous *Uh huhs*, and *Oh, I agrees*.

Eager to see just how far Miss Evans would carry this barking annoyance, his lordship waited until she had disconnected and stowed the phone, then rising he said, "My apologies please. I must attend to something." He had wanted to draw Emma out for a walk, see how the peach buds were wakening, but he knew she had to be hostess for Miss Evans, and he could not bear more of Miss Evans' company right now (someone had to tell that woman to leave her phone in her room), and, after offering a bite of bacon to Schrödinger perched on his tower, and a glance of regret to Emma, his lordship abruptly left the room.

The next days were able to pass in an equable manner with Lord Haversham spending some of them in London, while Emma and Brenda visited the village shops, orchards and greenhouse. Evenings, his lordship made certain to be back to spend time with Emma. When Miss Evans would need to go to her room for personal reasons, he would pull Emma into the library and lock the door. It was unspoken between them—the error of having Miss Evans at the manor. Lord Haversham wished Miss Evans would be called to return to the States. She interrupted whatever he said to the point where he began to say very little when she was near. And she asked him or John, whoever was around, personal questions. He couldn't trust her—she insisted on pushing her stateside boyfriend, Luke, who phoned only her, off on Emma, and her lack of manners were further evidenced by her answering her phone in the drawing room at tea.

The aroma of hyacinths preceded Brenda into the drawing room where Lord Haversham, Emma, John Britely, Lady Mardling, and Lady Southway, were seated awaiting lunch. They looked up to see Brenda carrying a tray ladened with small pots, each holding a pastel-hued bloom. Brenda's face gleamed with expectation.

No one spoke.

"I remember an article about Elizabeth Taylor," she said, "wherein it stated that she had fresh flowers brought in each day, for *each* room of her penthouse, straight from a Manhattan florist. She couldn't abide day-old blooms. I found these in the greenhouse." Brenda set the tray on a table, clapped her hands before her, and looked around for praise. The stillness about the room held steady.

Lord Haversham hardly roused; his facility for being good-natured had temporarily worn thin. Lady Mardling saved him, however, from attempting to be a good host, for, head back, looking down her nose, she said, "That sounds American, that article. Hollywood crazed." She flicked about a white handkerchief as she spoke and focused on his lordship. "I'm sure Simon's staff is equal to the task of supplying flowers throughout the manor. Indeed, I believe, unlike the Americans, his flowers are cut from his grounds, when in season, not from a florist."

"Oh," Brenda said. "It was something wonderful to do, gather these. Something exquisite to do." Hoping for a smile of understanding, she looked at his lordship.

"I've seen, my dear," Lady Mardling said, "that you have to be busy about. So typical."

14

"Typical? Typical of what, Lady Mardling?"

But before Lady Mardling could mold an apt reply, Brooks announced that lunch was served in the garden room; no one wanted to hear what Lady Mardling might say.

By now, it was understood that Emma's place at table was on Simon's right, and Simon nodded to Emma as he pulled out her chair. But there was some confusion over the chair to his left, and no one was to sit at the foot. If anyone were allowed to take the foot, Simon wanted it to be Emma. But, for now he preferred to have her by his side. His six weeks at Lake Como when she was in New York—when he had missed her so keenly, not knowing what her feelings were—had tightened his need, and just for now, he would keep her as near as he could. His eyes told her this, and his words, lest there be doubt. Lady Mardling and Brenda both jockeyed for Simon's left side position. Brooks pulled out the chair and looked at the women with a question.

"Lady Mardling, please sit here. We must respect your seniority," his lordship said, gesturing to the seat.

Was this an honor, Lady Mardling wondered. But she took the seat and Britely took the next. Brooks held the chair on Emma's right and said, "Miss Evans." And Brenda was left with no choice but to walk around to the other side of the table.

Their plates had been served and eating began in earnest. No one ventured to interrupt the soft clicking of forks until Lord Haversham said, "I suggest a day in London tomorrow. We can take in a museum and have lunch." He looked to Emma for her reaction.

"Oh, perfect!" Emma said. "Sound good to you, Brenda?"

Brenda's reply bypassed Emma altogether as it oozed down the table and wrapped around Simon. Her eyes held him tightly "Simon! How thoughtful." She intended now to use his given name more, although he had made it clear he did not welcome the familiarity.

It was becoming easier for him to ignore Miss Evans, and he continued to look at Emma, and then to John Britely. "John, please join us. We'd like your company, and indeed, you're a better driver than I. You can drive us in."

The next day after an early breakfast, they gathered at the front terrace where John Britely waited with the Bentley. As Hadley held the front passenger door open for her, Lord Haversham said, "Miss Evans, you should sit in front with Mr. Britely where you will have the best view of the landscape." Instead, Brenda slid into the back seat, and, patting the seat next to her, said, "Simon, sit here, there's so much I want to ask you about the history of the villages we pass. Please be my tour guide."

His lordship seemed unable to move. He looked at Emma. Time hung for a second waiting for what was to occur now. Brenda arranged her skirt over her chiseled knees in just a certain way, and leaned over to look up at Simon standing there.

Emma had to arrange her thoughts before she could yield and say, "Do sit there, Simon. Join Brenda so you can more easily be her tour guide."

"Right . . . right," he said, though he sounded reluctant, and he waited for Emma to take her seat in front. He then slid into the Bentley next to Brenda. They were on their way with a less than satisfied Lord Haversham. As the fields and history rolled by, Brenda heard only half of his lordship's commentary.

"This field, on the right," he said, "is the site of one of King William III's battles during the Civil War in the late 17th century."

Brenda looked at Simon, not at the field. She heard his strong, rounded voice, not his words; he could have been expounding on the virtues of spaghetti. Emma had said that Lord Haversham was a commanding presence, but Brenda hadn't expected this voice, these intense, vital eyes, his flat stomach. She wanted to put her hand there; instead for half a second, she put her hand on Simon's leg—a second so brief he had no time to react. But his next word was delayed, caught in his throat.

The Bentley seemed to float; John maneuverer it with love while he and Emma silently watched the interesting landscape roll by. John knew the terrain, every blade, he thought, and by now Emma knew it fairly well herself. Other than a short comment to each other now and then, there was no need for them to speak, just listen to the fine automobile and to their thoughts. Nothing to do but hear the childish questions, prattle, and pandering with which Brenda continued to assault his lordship. Emma heard the thinning chord of Simon's patience.

As for himself, Lord Haversham tried to be a good host, amiably pointing out landmarks, but the silliness of this guest, and the more she applied the pressure of her thigh to his, the more he vowed to himself to avoid her from now on except for meals, and he would miss more of those if he could. He had moved more to his side of the seat, but somehow, Miss Evans found a slant, or turn, to work her way again nearer him. Soon, if Miss Evans didn't return to the States, he would take Emma somewhere and tell Miss Evans that she had to leave, that the manor was to be closed. This would disrupt the lives of his staff, the life of the manor, and even the public, some of whom came to the village of Cav Neumont purposely to see the manor. Even so, he felt that desperate. He thought of Miss Evans' presence as wearing on him like a crown of thorns.

The remainder of the day went rather in that manner, with his lordship taking Emma's arm when he could as they proceeded through the British Museum, and Miss Evans often laying claim to his other arm. He longed for the sanctity of his library at the manor. He had thoughts about the way with which he had disposed of his ex-wife, Lady Claire Haversham, Peter's mother. Following their divorce, he had set her up in a London town home after she had become a financial problem for him by running up debts, gambling, running around the globe until it constituted abandonment. But he was not responsible for this American; he would find a way to ship her home. He would gladly be responsible for Emma, if she would let him. It was too early to know, though he knew she deeply shared his love. There it was: *love*.

When they arrived back at the manor, Lord Haversham announced that he would take a tray in his room. But off to the side, he asked Brooks to serve Emma and him in his private study, an above-stairs room that connected his bedroom to Solar, Emma's bedroom. He told John he had to get away from that woman; please excuse him from dinner. He didn't provide reasons to Miss Evans about his and Emma's absence at dinner; let her think what she would.

He said to Emma, "I don't know what answer you are to give Miss Evans when she asks you where you were at dinner, as she is sure to do."

Emma touched his cheek and smiled. She felt that she couldn't take Brenda seriously. True, she thought, Brenda was proving to be a nuisance, but she would soon be gone, and Simon and she could look forward to that. "Perhaps I'll find a little white lie; I think the situation calls for one."

And so they dined in peace at a small table by a window that gave onto the lighted terrace below.

III

Lord Haversham Must be in London

Schrödinger waited on his perch for the group to assemble around the breakfast table. Normally seating was informal with each hungry breakfaster coming down as he or she was ready. Somehow, Lord Haversham and Emma always managed to arrive about the same time. He would hold out her chair for her, then take his seat. Brooks would already have placed the morning paper near his lordship, but he would not open it when Emma was there. Instead, he would tell her how pretty she was, and how special he felt to be able to start his morning with her in view. She would thank him and say how pleasant this was, or how she enjoyed the view through the tall French windows, and how his Haversham ancestors had so cleverly arranged this lovely breakfast room to look through those windows out onto a garden, and how smart for them to have arranged the ancient flower beds there. Even though these mornings were always misty and grey, spring blooms had arranged themselves into mauves and pale yellows. So fitting. When he would watch Emma taking in that view, Lord Haversham's pride rose up into feeling that it was he alone who had provided such beauty, and just for her. He felt as though he had personally molded each petal.

This morning all were assembled at about the same time as usual. Emma didn't want to miss Simon, he didn't want to miss her; John Britely had early work to attend to with the accounts, and Brenda didn't want to miss anything that had to do with Simon.

He had news. "I must be in London today, back tomorrow," he said. He scanned the group. He wanted to invite Emma to join him, but, alas, she had to entertain Miss Evans, and there was very little that could induce him to spend another day trapped with Miss Evans. "I'd like to invite you to join me," he looked at Emma, "but I'm afraid I won't be able to spend time with you. I have meetings with several members of the Cabinet." He released a long sigh for Emma. "One must do one's duty for the country."

"There's so much to do and see here," Emma said. "Though unwilling, we'll be content without your presence."

Brenda's brow tightened up into disappointment; her response burst out without restraint. "Simon, I'd love to go. Couldn't it be worked out?"

A scowl crossed Lord Haversham's brow. He would not respond.

Emma turned to Brenda. "He'll be busy, and even though we're self-sufficient, he would worry about us, have to watch the time and all." Her *us* was meant to make it clear that, in any case, Brenda was not to go alone with Simon. "We'll write and read before the fire, walk about in all directions to enjoy spring blooms, walk to the village. There is so much here to do," she said. Then remembering that Brenda resisted that walk, "Or perhaps Hadley could bring around a golf cart and we can ride there. We won't be at a loss for activity. Sad to say, Simon."

"Ah, it's true then," he said. "My presence plays but a peripheral role. Just as I feared," he laughed.

"Oh, not so, Simon," Brenda said. "Your presence is central."

Lord Haversham avoided the gaze that Brenda arched across the table to him.

"So true," Emma said. "We only need you for a tour guide, Simon." But the warm look she gave him belied her intent.

IV

Emma Meets the London Law Firm

Mist steadied in its purpose to stick around, letting taupe, the color for this day, hang outside the French windows. Even so, a feeling of spring lay about in a more focused way. On the previous day Simon had completed his duty in London, returning late, and Emma had waited up for him. Brenda stayed in her room, as she had been told that no one was likely to be about except for, possibly, the ghost, Lady Joan. Thus, Emma and Lord Haversham were able to have a nightcap together. They were largely silent, not needing words to show pleasure in each other's company. Then he had walked her to her room and held on to her—unwilling to part so soon.

"The day will come," he had said, "and not too long from now . . .." The remainder of his meaning had hung in the air unspoken, and as he spoke, his words and smile wrapped around Emma. Taking time to build a union between a man and a woman conferred emotional strength. He knew that, and he knew she felt the same. He had kissed her hard, and let her slip into her room. He hardly felt the floor as he walked down to his room.

Thoughts of Simon, his kiss, his arms, had kept Emma company as she fell into a deep, nurturing sleep.

At breakfast, Sir Simon, Emma, and John Britely talked about plans for the day. Simon and John would be in conference with carpenters, and something had to be done about the pool, which needed repairs before the heat could be turned on. The grounds man would be in for a meeting and a stonemason would be around to bolster some wobbly quoining. The ancient manor was always as needy as a babe in nappies. Emma had an appointment in London to introduce her to the law firm with which Tortle and Gainer would be consulting.

Brenda arrived at breakfast in a garment that slouched like pyjamas. His lordship wasn't certain, but perhaps it was an American style. Besides he understood it was not easy to pack an adequate wardrobe in a backpack; he would make allowances. (He hadn't seen her many suitcases.)

"Good morning," she said, looking around at those assembled. Brooks lifted lids for her while she dished eggs and kippers onto a plate. Then she took her usual seat to Simon's left, next to John Britely. Brooks poured her coffee.

"Thank you, Brooks," Simon said. "Miss Evans," he continued, "you'll be left to your own devices today. You know that Emma has an appointment in London, and Mr. Britely and I will be busy with estate repairmen and such. We'll all have a long, busy, day of it. Hadley or Brooks and cook will see to your comfort, and that you dine well. There is a roaring fire for you in the library." Brenda looked at him as though his words were holy. Though her face was lovely, Simon had to look away—so directly did it bore into him that it might as well be sharp-edged stone. Looking at Emma made much more sense. Hers was the face he had come to adore. He had grown to enjoy her intelligent contribution, always there but never pushed. She never imposed—allowed him room to pursue. He thought that he and she walked in lock step. Perhaps even knew each other's thoughts. "The mist is expected to clear in an hour or so, and you can walk about," he said. "The orchards are lovely, just popping their buds. And we'll all be together for dinner."

"Emma, I'll take you to the train," he continued. "Every moment spent with you is my pleasure. Let me know when you're ready to leave. And on your return, please give me a call so I'll know which train to meet."

"Simon, might I come with you to the train?" Brenda asked. "I love that ride and it will help break up my day."

For an instant, Lord Haversham had dark thoughts: in his mind, he saw a vision—Lady Joan providing a service—scaring this intrusive woman back to the States. For a brief second, he wondered whether he could train Lady Joan to come when he beckoned. However, lacking Lady Joan, he still would not let Miss Evans impose. "I am afraid not. I'll have some stops to make afterward. I don't know how long I'll be detained." Indeed, he could fabricate when he had to, when he felt squeezed. "I'm sure you can sufficiently entertain yourself, there is much to do here." Then he thought about Emma: he must tread lightly in reference to their dreadful guest. Although he knew that as well, Emma found Miss Evans' behavior to be appalling—for reasons of her own Emma might have to work again in New York with Miss Evans; he didn't want to embarrass Emma. "And Hadley can bring around a bicycle should you want to ride to the village. Have you found our excellent stationers and bookstore?"

Brenda seemed suitably blocked for the while; even so she might find a way to spend some time alone with his lordship. It would be lovely to be his favorite; to receive the attention he was giving Emma. He had to eat lunch; perhaps she could find a way to join him. "Well, I'll look for you at lunch then." With her head at a becoming angle that she had been told was her best, her smile wore into him.

Lord Haversham gasped, he nearly showed his anger, "Ah . . . not convenient, Miss Evans. Mr. Britely and I will be having a working lunch, discussing repairs with roofers." Another fabrication, born in a second. He was beginning to excel at these spontaneous prevarications. And poor John—here he was speaking for him. John wouldn't want a working lunch. He preferred his breaks. Indeed, well deserved them.

During these exchanges, Emma and John maintained an interest in their breakfast—more of an interest than usual, trying not to look at Brenda or his lordship as he struggled to keep his composure against Brenda's onslaughts.

John Britely listened with amusement. He had witnessed his lordship's expert parrying of Lady Mardling's and Lady Southway's barbs; he had admired his performance as he kept his former wife, Lady Claire from meddling, and now he listened with pleasure while his lordship danced avoidance around this astonishing American. Lord Haversham could always amaze, often had a surprise to pull out, to evoke when pressed. Between watching and listening to the women, and now Miss Evans, there was plenty to entertain at Cav Neumont Manor.

Emma listened—happy that Simon had drawn the morning in a way that he and she could ride to the train, just the two of them. With Brenda always around, there had not been enough bits and pieces of moments with Simon at a time when they had just barely gotten to know each other. He would take her hand and tighten his hand around it, but it felt awkward in front of Miss Evans. When Simon had been so quick to invite Miss Evans over, they hadn't foreseen the restraint her presence would confer. Perhaps Brenda would go home soon, Emma thought. Didn't she have to work? Didn't she miss Luke? Would Simon arrange a scheme to send her home? It was not easy.

"How is Luke managing without you?" Emma asked. Perhaps that would pull out information, let them know when Brenda had to return to the States and to work. But again Brenda's response was inappropriate.

"Oh, you're the one he misses. Hasn't he called you?" Brenda said, giving a knowing glance to Simon.

"No, actually, he and I haven't spoken since I left there several weeks ago. There's nothing between him and me. Surely you must know that."

"Oh, I had the impression that he was calling you."

"I don't know why he would. He and I barely crossed paths at work. Isn't he on your team?"

"He *was*," Brenda said with such finality—let there be no doubt—he isn't now.

Emma wanted to stop this repartee. Not only did she not understand Brenda's position, but as well, she was surprised at it, surprised at Brenda's attitude. And now she had the upcoming London meeting for which to prepare questions and answers. And although she would be employed by Tortle and Gainer, an Arizona law firm, the London firm for which Tortle would be consulting wanted to meet Tortle's employees. Simon and she had discussed that when she started on the contract, he would spend time with her in London during the week. Then, if she were free, she would come to the manor at week's end. She looked forward to this arrangement as well as to the challenge of seeing the law from the other side of the ocean. She enjoyed her work, her paralegal skills thrived on the challenge.

"I see," Emma said. "Well, he certainly isn't calling me, nor would I expect him to."

To this Brenda merely formed a disparaging huh, tucking on a little side sneer.

Emma had a good day in London. Greg Tortle toured her around the offices, and introduced her to the principals with whom she would work, and who, after the meeting, took Simon and Emma to lunch at their club. The firm held a bank of hotel rooms for its visitors and consultants, and in the afternoon, Emma was shown one of the hotel rooms that would be reserved for her, and then Greg took her to the train. The train would take her to Benning's Turn; then, unless she called Simon, she would have to get a bus to Cav Neumont. It was early enough when she arrived, that a call to Simon wouldn't be disruptive, and she made the call.

Brenda, however, had been watching the front terrace to catch him leaving and when she saw the Morgan brought around, she flew across the hall and down the steps. "I'd like to ride along, Simon."

He looked at her with an astonishment that would scare off a breeze. The elements held their breath to see what would happen next. Then he took his seat in the car and without a word, firmly shut its door and drove off leaving Miss Evans standing there wearing disappointment. As he sped out and down the lane, he wished that on his return with Emma, Miss Evans would be a pillar of salt.

V

Rage

Brenda and Emma stepped along avoiding downed branches and twigs. The narrow trail required walking in tandem and Brenda led. It was her idea to take the ungroomed Bingers public path that due to its narrowness and sudden drop-offs was an unfrequented hike. You had to watch your head as well, for here and there branches claimed a position across the open space. Emma had warned her about Bingers' hazards. And yet, Brenda said she must see those acres of bluebells, now at their prime, about which she had heard so much. Emma felt optimistic— Brenda seemed less moody today, had asked her to hike, and had gotten over her aversion for walking. Perhaps whatever had been bothering her was settled or forgotten. Emma couldn't imagine what it could have been, but clearly Brenda hadn't been the friendly sort as she had been back at work in the States.

They had left the manor by way of the south wing, a terrace entrance not frequented often, and which led toward the direction of Bingers. They carried water, rolls and cheese in their waist packs, and to steady their way they took thick hiking sticks that they had found stored inside a stand in the hallway. When they had walked for about two hours, pushing branches this way and that, crunching growth with their boots, they saw off to the south a vast field of bluebells that lay thick and undisturbed, intertwined between tree trunks. When clouds opened, the bells worked to catch spots of sun—a weak sun, but just enough on this chilly day. Their strong, shimmering blue color seemed to rise up filling the atmosphere.

"I want to walk over through the bluebells," Brenda said. She stopped in the path and looked toward the layer of blue that began about thirty meters away.

The steps through to the edge of that blue layer looked risky and would be uncertain, soft, insecure footing. But Brenda, ducking branches, took the first steps in that direction. Emma followed. When the women reached the unknitted edges of blue, Brenda continued tramping into the bluebells' midst. "Come," she said. "I want to be surrounded."

Emma threaded her way behind Brenda and soon a thick fabric of blue surrounded them, brushing against their ankles. Wings fluttered around them, disrupted by this unusual trespass. When Emma looked back, the view of the trail was closed off by trees, weeds, downed leaves, bushes, and limbs that they had picked their way through. Had they not known exactly where the trail lay, they would have been lost. They stopped now to feel this marvelous place.

"Surely this is the field Simon mentioned," Brenda said. "He said it was hard to reach because the landowner doesn't keep the trail cleared."

"Yes. That's true," Emma said. She had had a disastrous encounter with Bingers on her previous trip to Cav Neumont when she had slipped on wet leaves and taken a plunge down a cliff where she was stranded for three days.

The sky threatened to pull back its light, and if they turned back now, they would be just in time for tea. Emma looked at Brenda with a question—was she ready to pick up the trail? Head back? She was surprised to see Brenda stiffening, rigid, lips thinned straight into a line, face pulled into tight eyes. She had not before seen that surprising, threatening mask on Brenda. Seconds of silence stood between them.

"I dare say no one has ever been standing exactly here," Brenda said. "At least not since the Romans marched through and settled." The statement was angry, forced through teeth.

"Indeed, not even Romans. Their horses would have had a hard time of it on Bingers . . . they would have come through the valley. This is likely the most isolated spot in southern England."

"Right. Let's turn back. We've been out two hours now. We'll arrive back just in time for tea."

And they turned to trace their way back. Now Brenda followed Emma. Brenda had purposely picked the heaviest hiking stick in the stand, and though it had been a bit heavy to place as she moved along Bingers, it would serve its duty now, and she pulled the stick up with both hands and brought it down sharp and hard, squarely onto that central crown of silken curls topping Emma's skull—the hair that she had seen Lord Haversham gaze at so often and sometimes to reach out and touch when he thought no one was looking. Then again. And once more a blow to the side of Emma's face where it lay, partly covered by bluebells.

Emma lay still.

For a moment Brenda lingered over—watching her. She saw that Emma's body quivered, and then did not move again. Not a twitch. No breath in or out. A trickle of blood ran out of her ear. She looked peaceful though. Brenda thought that what she had done wasn't so bad after all; Emma really had not much purpose in life, her son Josh was fairly grown, and essentially Emma had no responsibilities. She waited a few seconds, then leaned over Emma's form, careful not to crush more flowers, and began to inch out Emma's waist pack. She removed her passport, wallet, and cell phone, picked up her stick, then threaded her way through the flowers until she was about fifteen meters from Emma, and by using one of the hiking sticks, she wedged a hole into the soft loam, and dropped in Emma's things. Then she pushed the soil back over them, tamping it down firmly. She knew that those items would be easy to find if someone knew where to look, but no one would ever be there. She knew that. And in time if someone did find Emma's body there would be no identification. She looked toward where Emma lay and all was still. Even the planet seemed to be still as it tried to assimilate what had just happened. Carrying both sticks,

Brenda picked her way to the path, then turned to look where Emma lay, to verify that from the path, nothing could be seen. The way back was easier and she swiftly moved along Bingers toward the manor and to tea. She had laid the groundwork for her plan. She had been surprised on first meeting Lord Haversham; surprised at his attractiveness. She had pictured an old codger. Emma had said he was very pleasant, and now that Brenda knew, she couldn't rest without creating a path to him for herself. Her plan would take time, but she was up for it, and as she walked back, her step had an optimistic bounce.

But no matter how carefully she shaped her journey to his lordship, she would forever be out of step.

She came into the manor through the south hall and placed both sticks into the stand. Before coming in she had wiped off hers so that it was quite clean, no sign of blood. She threaded her way through the many hallways up to her room to change for tea. There was something else she must do before going down. All her way back from the hike, she had reviewed the fine details necessary to advance her plan: for one, she must go to Emma's room and remove some of her things. It would make her slightly late for tea, but now was the perfect time while everyone was downstairs. Even Ellie and Mrs. Penrose would be down for tea with the staff. But she must hurry. She quietly rushed down the hall turning onto Emma's hall, and into Emma's room where she quickly put the laptop and a few pieces of clothing into Emma's backpack and returned to her own room with those items, hiding them in her closet. Another part of her plan was getting rid of Emma's backpack, and she had thought of a way to do that. Then she coolly walked down to the drawing room where tea was just now being served.

Lady Mardling, Lady Southway, and Sophia Bachman were assembled around the ever-present fire, discussing an upcoming farmers' market. His lordship and John Britely listened on, wondering exactly what would be their role in the affair. Likely as not, the women had a scheme going that would include the men. Brooks laid a log on and poked the fire while Lady Mardling poured out a cup and handed it to Brenda.

"And which trail did you explore today, Miss Evans?" Lady Mardling asked.

"Neumont path," Brenda said. Her face easily camouflaged this lie. Then she remembered that had she and Emma actually planned to go along Neumont, they would have left and returned from the front of the manor, not the south wing. But surely no one had noticed.

Lord Haversham expected Emma to come in for tea and after empty minutes listening to gossip threads winding among those assembled, and still no Emma, he said to Brenda, "Miss Evans, where is Ms. Chapman? Didn't she hike with you?"

"Indeed, we did start out together, but early on she said that she wanted to go to the stationers for a new journal, and she turned toward the village. I expect that she got busy among the shops, and forgot the time. She'll be along shortly, I'm certain." This would be her firm story. How could anyone say differently?

But Emma didn't arrive. She missed tea altogether, and by dinner, when she didn't appear, Lord Haversham, John, Brooks, and two more of the staff walked in different directions in search of her, asking all they met whether she had been seen. His lordship dialed her mobile repeatedly without an answer.

LORD HAVERSHAM SPENT a sleepless night, and the next morning he could eat no breakfast; indeed, he could not even sit, and he paced from room to room, head bent in worry. He hardly heard if someone spoke to him. And when shops opened, he and John asked at every shop. No one recalled seeing a woman who fitted Emma's description, not even the stationer. "No one bought a journal yesterday," the stationer said. "I know the American, she's been in several times, and I'm certain she wasn't in here yesterday."

Lord Haversham called the police. In fact, he went in to their office to speak directly to Detective Chief Inspector Adams, a fine officer whom his lordship had known for years. "You may have seen Ms. Chapman about town, Chief Inspector. She's been a guest at the manor for several weeks recently, as well as during last fall. She's quite stable, grounded, and regular in her habits. I know her to be responsible and dependable, not at all hysterical. This absence is not like her, and I couldn't be more worried."

DCI Adams understood. He saw the worry binding his lordship's face. He would put all the forces of this and surrounding towns in search of Ms. Emma Chapman. Bus drivers and shopkeepers would be questioned immediately, and if Ms. Chapman didn't turn up in a day or two, and hadn't sent word, he would spread his net farther. She had to be somewhere and he would bring the force of England's finest to the pursuit. However, did Ms. Chapman want to be missing? Though it wasn't considerate, occasionally people do go off without notice. He could only wonder. Perhaps the bus driver would remember taking her to the train. But after three days, there had still been no sign of a woman who may have been Emma Chapman.

"She must have quickly slipped through their net," Brenda was heard to say. "I thought she carried an unusually large backpack to go hiking." Surely, she thought, no one had seen Emma leave for the hike wearing only a small waist pack.

Finally, his lordship and Mrs. Penrose looked in Emma's room to see if her things were gone. They found a few items of clothing, but no backpack or laptop, and sitting on her bed table was the gold clock he had given her. Most odd, he thought.

At dinner, Brenda was hard-put to get a conversation going. Lord Haversham could barely respond to any remark—usually not at all. John Britely was glum as well. His lordship wished he could grieve alone; he wished Miss Evans would go home. He had discouraged Lady Mardling from dropping in by saying he wasn't entertaining; he would not discuss Emma's absence with Lady Mardling—he could imaging her acerbic remarks. And when she invited him to dine at her chateau, he replied that such was impossible at this time. He hardly felt like eating, but Brooks managed to get his lordship to come to table for at least a bowl of soup.

Brenda elected to drop her little bomb, one she had been planning and had rehearsed to herself. She knew it would hurt Simon, but he would get over it and soon—with her help. While trying not to show pleasure, she started, "I haven't wanted to mention it, but now I am afraid I must—several times Emma told me that she wasn't looking forward to working in London. She hinted that she wanted to go home. Perhaps that's what she did." Interpreting the frosty look of disbelief that Lord Haversham turned on her, chilled Brenda, but only for a few seconds.

Emma didn't hint. Simon knew that about her character. Her truth was always ready at hand. If she had wanted to go home, he would have known; as it was, he knew she wanted to be with him, had been pleased to take the contract in London, had been pleased to join him there afterhours. He could see her eyes lighting up at the sight of him. No. This story Miss Evans told was not Emma. Her tale could not have been less painful for his knowing how unlikely it was. But what could he think? Emma wasn't here. His insides gnashed as he studied his glass, gently twirling it about. He turned to study the fire while observing Miss Evans peripherally. Did she seem certain? He could see that she was nervously twisting her fingers together.

Life at the manor now became suspended as though stuck in glue, immobile. Greg Tortle called Lord Haversham, "Sir Simon, I haven't been able to reach Emma. She doesn't answer her mobile, and I want to go over some features with her about the London contract." He waited so long for Lord Haversham's reply that he almost asked, *Are you there*?

His lordship didn't want to discuss Emma at all, but he could almost hear her telling him how much she respected Mr. Tortle, and so he said, "Sadly, Greg, she's not here—we've not heard from her either and have no idea where she is. She just suddenly didn't return from a hike, and apparently, she's taken a few of her things with her. If we learn anything, I'll give you a call."

VI

Emma Wakes in Bluebells

Emma was afraid to open her eyes. She listened to faint rustlings around her trying to resolve the sounds: what were they? From where? Murmurings. Grasses? Trees? She felt other-worldly, disoriented, dizzy. She gathered strength from somewhere deep inside her spirit and slowly opened one eye; the other wouldn't open. Clouds. She could see clouds; could see them better if they would be still; stop rotating. Something moved along her arm. She turned her head to see whether she could make it out, whether she could focus. Slowly the image became clearer and she saw that it was a bluebell. Bluebells were making the sound, talking amongst themselves. But why was she here? How did she get here? As her focus sharpened, a pain in her head sharpened as well. She pulled in a deep breath and tried to think beyond the pain. What to do? She shouldn't be lying here; she was thirsty, her face throbbed, her skull throbbed, she touched her eye and then her cheek and found what looked like dried blood on her finger. With great effort she roused to sit and look around. In all directions were only trees, brush, and a meadow of bluebells. *Bluebells*. She had to move. She pulled herself to her feet, and now her head was seriously throbbing. Unsteady, she worked to balance herself, to stand still, to look around. Then she noticed the fanny pack around her waist and inside it found a roll, and cheese and water. The food was dried and stale, but she ate greedily. With her energy restored a bit, she thought she could walk. But which way? Walk? What else could she do? Walk to something, anything. She must have business somewhere, know someone, somewhere. She must try to find a road, and looking around, she thought she saw a clearing in the trees. She would find out what was there—a cottage perhaps. But when she managed to wade through the bluebells to the clearing, she saw that it was only a trail and not a wide one, but nevertheless it must lead somewhere. Perhaps that was where she had come from, or where she was heading. And with a throbbing head that made it hard to think, she started up the trail.

VII

DCI Adams Interviews Brenda

"Miss Evans, please tell me again why Ms. Chapman wandered off," DCI Adams said, as he consulted his notes.

"Well, I don't know. She wanted to walk through dense brush to see something, a blossom or something that I had no interest in, and so I said that I would wait there for her, and I sat down on a log. I had my back to her and paid no attention to what she did, expecting her to come back in a few minutes."

"Miss Evans, you said previously that she left for the village to buy a journal." A sensitive man, the detective could be uncomfortable grilling a beautiful woman such as this one before him, but he had years of experience to draw on and he would not hesitate to drill down as needed.

"That's true. I think that was when she left. I was so tired by that time . . . not used to so much hiking . . . I'm not clear."

"What was she carrying with her?" DCI Adams asked.

"A backpack. I wondered why she hadn't worn just a small waist pack which would have been adequate for the water and snack we carried."

"Do you think she had identification with her? Her billfold? Passport?"

"Hmm . . . no idea. Before we left, she said she had to go to her room for a minute. I don't know why."

"Perhaps to pick up her backpack?"

"I guess that could have been the reason."

"On the trail, did you call out to her when she didn't return?"

"Oh yes. I called repeatedly and looked over in the direction where she had headed. I couldn't see anything higher than a cow's tail. The brush, though thick and scratchy, was fairly low. Off in the distance I thought I could see a road. Maybe she headed there thinking it would be a shortcut to the village."

"Miss Evans, if she told you she was leaving, or going to the village for a journal, why did you keep calling her?"

For a second, Brenda was caught. Then, "I was concerned about her striking out alone."

"But she didn't reply?"

"No. And she was quickly out of sight. I thought that she must know the area well."

"Did she seem to be okay?"

"Yes. Perfectly. Otherwise I wouldn't have expected her to walk out as vigorously as she did. I'm still surprised at her willingness to leave me alone."

"How did you know that she was quickly out of sight when you had your back to her?"

"Well . . ." Brenda realized she had to slow down and think about her answers more carefully. In half-a-minute, she said, "I did look around for her."

"I see. Can you think of a reason she would want to disappear?"

Brenda thought through her reply. "She's been reluctant to take the case in London. She said that she would be the lead paralegal and often that meant that she would have to carry the workload of others." None of this was true, but she would defy anyone to know exactly what Emma said to her in private.

"I see," DCI Adams said, taking notes.

"Also," Brenda continued, "she said she missed Luke, one of the guys in the New York firm." She looked at his lordship as she let that hang in the air. Water the seed. It was too far across the pond, even in this day of instant communication, for anyone to know that this was pure fabrication, that Luke belonged to herself—if she wanted him.

Lord Haversham's brow knotted into a mixture of pain and disbelief.

"Did she have any other personal issues that you know of?" DCI Adams asked.

"I think she just wanted to go home . . . or to get away to an island. Actually, she mentioned an island, Utila, I think, but perhaps not seriously." As Brenda paused to weigh her next remark, she looked at Lord Haversham again. "And she said she had heard from Luke and that he had spoken about their future. She was excited about that." Brenda amazed herself with the ploy she had quickly brought up; amazed at how easily stories could multiply. She noticed Simon's confusion. Progress, she thought.

"Miss Evans," DCI Adams studied his notes, flipping pages back and forth, while he attempted to pull together discrepancies, "please excuse me, but I am bewildered about what Ms. Chapman said to you: a). Ms. Chapman did not like the London assignment; b) wanted to go buy a journal; c) wanted to go home; d) had something going on back in the States with someone named Luke; and e) mentioned getting away, going to an island. Which of these dreams or discontents do you think most likely applies to Ms. Chapman?" He flapped his notebook on his knee and studied Brenda, his eyes raised under his lowered head.

Brenda nearly stuttered, her cavalier cheerfulness deserting her. "I don't know. I guess Emma's confused state has confused me. Her uncertainty has caused mine."

DCI Adams closed his notebook with a loud snap and turned to Lord Haversham. The two men swapped perplexed looks. The detective pocketed his notebook, and while he reviewed his internal dialogue, looking off into space for clarity, Lord Haversham waited. The ever-attentive Brooks refilled their cups. Brenda kept a pasted worried expression in force, and when the detective glanced at her from time to time, he wondered about that expression. Based on all the thousand expressions that had passed before his eyes over the years, it wasn't quite genuine somehow; told a story different from those issuing from her mouth. He saw that Lord Haversham's expression was pure grief; the man was hurting.

DCI Adams drained his cup, set it down and looked at his lordship. "I have no more questions for now. Please be available both of you, I may need to talk to you again."

"Indeed. I'll always be available," Lord Haversham said, "and I hope Emma will walk in any minute. I'm deeply concerned. She's a vital presence and we miss her. I can't imagine . . .," his voice trailed off. A thousand times now he had gone over any—over all—possible logical reasons Emma would suddenly leave.

"I think she was embarrassed about leaving, especially after all your kindness," Brenda said, looking at Simon. Brenda knew that he would eventually respond to her sympathy. She was more composed now, better able to explain. "And always having to say how she would enjoy the work, when in fact she knew she would hate it."

His lordship couldn't imagine Emma holding much hatred.

Brenda would stick with each of her stories about Emma's leaving. How could anyone say differently? Lord Haversham would be slightly heartbroken for a week or so, but she knew she could help him forget Emma; blessed with beauty, she had always had her pick of men. The detectives had zilch to go on; Emma could have left or could have been kidnapped, both options would have to be considered.

DCI Adams and his partner, DS Sanders, combed Emma's room at the manor and found no clues to explain her leaving. A few items of clothing and notebooks seemed in order. DCI Adams thumbed through the notebooks looking for any revealing message, but they held only notes that appeared to be for a novel in progress. Of interest to the detectives was the fact that they found no suitcase, backpack, or computer, and Lord Haversham had said that she used a laptop for writing her novel. Judging from the absence of those items, it would appear that she had planned to leave.

Now, the detectives had left, and Brenda waited at the tea table for his lordship's attention. But, instead, he said he needed time alone in his study, and he hoped she could find peace somehow for the rest of the afternoon. Brenda watched Brooks clear away the tea service, and then she was left sitting, gazing about the drawing room, alone but hopeful.

Even in the hard rain, Lord Haversham, strung with unrelieved stress, rode out on his fine horse, Bud, with Major trailing along beside. They returned soaked. Hadley wiped down Major, and then led Bud off to his warm stall. His lordship went up to his room for dry clothing, but returned still chilled throughout, body and soul. He couldn't speak about Emma; tried to keep his head in a book, not seeing the print, unable to sit still for more than a few minutes at a time. John Britely was forced to converse with Miss Evans. Both he and his lordship doubted her stories, but couldn't say so; wanted her to go home.

Lord Haversham thought of leaving; that would send Miss Evans home, but he could not leave—could not leave the last place he had seen Emma. She would yet return—he was certain. And anyway, DCI Adams had asked him and Miss Evans to stay. Curses. Miss Evans must be wrong; something had to have happened to Emma. Maybe Lady Joan could locate Emma. Indeed, she had been around more lately, seemed agitated, stirring about. He moved closer to the fire, trying to warm the chill shaking him. Not only his soul, but also his bones were rattling. Some days he sought solace in the manor's chapel, but those old stones gave one a cold reception, and after he had endured it long enough to send up a prayer, concentrating on Emma's safety and return, he would leave quite frozen and stiff, fingers blue.

VIII

What Brenda Had to Do

Although his lordship hadn't felt well lately, his signature was needed on documents in London and he had asked John Britely to drive him in. Left to her own devices, it was a good day for Brenda to do what she had to do. She was expected to read or write letters and walk about the orchards until lunch when cook would have a salad ready for her in the garden room. Then it was thought that she could write more letters and walk about some more until tea, which Brooks would serve for her in the library, then she was expected to walk about more until dinner was announced, at which time Simon and John should be back from London.

But she had something more pressing to do. She took Emma's backpack from her closet, checked to see that Emma's laptop was still there along with a few pieces of clothing, removed the laptop, booted it up, and deleted as much of its contents as she could, reformatting the hard drive as well. Then she returned it to the backpack, put on sneakers, shouldered the bag and set off for the bus stop in the village. It would be about five miles, taking the short cut behind the village green, to the bus, but she knew she could do that in less than an hour-and-a-half. She could do it now, used to more walking

About halfway along the road, she stopped and removed Emma's laptop from the backpack. Then removing a disk from the drive, she scraped it up with a pebble, broke it into pieces, and tossed them under a dense hedge. Finally, she brought her hiking stick hard down on the computer until it was fractured in numerous places. Her anger decreased with each blow; she finally felt satisfaction. This life: this manor life, this life with Simon was what she had always sought in her dreams, read about in novels, and fate had brought that very situation so close to her that all she had left to do was wait, try to be patient—Simon was not one to jump into romantic situations. There were no other contenders; she had studied the social terrain. Time would work its magic.

At the bus stop she bought a roundtrip ticket for Chipping Campden—that would get her back to Cav Neumont in time to walk the five miles to the manor, arriving at dinnertime. If anyone saw her, they would think nothing of a woman with a backpack. That it was Emma's and not hers was the key, but no one would know the distinction.

The ride to Chipping Campden provided time for her to dream about Simon. She thought he was starting to accept that Emma had wanted to leave, and had in fact decided to leave. Emma left all right; she herself saw to that. Sometimes in life, it was true that fate was standing by waiting for orders. She had learned that when her stepmother had taken her into her own harsh hands until she kicked bloody hell out of her. That had taught her. Since then she had learned that it was necessary to teach others; teach them how to treat you, and if they didn't learn, teach them how to get out of your way. But those like Emma—so sweet, sickeningly sweet, never in the way—were hard to teach, so she had had to do what she had done. And there was Simon, again hard to teach. Simon was hurting, but it would all turn out her way in the end. She knew how to soothe him.

In Chipping Campden Brenda stepped down from the bus and began her purposeful walk. If passers-by observed her, they would think she belonged there. She walked High Street, browsing shop windows, until in a side alley she saw exactly what she was looking for—a large trash bin. She removed the laptop from the backpack, then, with a struggle, she raised the heavy lid just enough to throw the laptop computer into the bin. Then she tossed Emma's backpack over the edge and heard it thunk inside. She looked around; no one was about. No windows hung over that alley, and no one had seen her. She had removed all identification from Emma's belongings, and if the pack and laptop were found, there would be no way to trace them back to her or to Emma. Chipping Campden was just large enough a town that mysterious trash would remain mysterious. This was her good deed for the day.

Back at the manor when she walked in to dinner, she said that she was sorry to come in a bit late without changing, but her enthusiastic walks through the orchards had proved so stimulating that she had lost track of time. And all in all, it seemed to have been a rewarding explanation—for Simon, for the first time, looked pleased at something she had done

But Lord Haversham's pleased look was the natural appearance he wore when he was completely drained. He felt ill, and shortly went off to bed.

IX

Mars Marsden Finds Emma

Mars Marsden opened the mudroom door and stepped out behind his dog, Harvey, to watch him light out for his morning run. Wonderful dog, solid member of the family, Harvey sprinted with the joy of brisk, fresh air, endless space, the best for running. Harvey cut through the gate, circled the back paddock, and frisked up to say hello to cows waiting at the trough. It was that time of early morning. But then Harvey diverted from his usual romp, ducked back out of the field and sprinted off toward the front fence. Where was he headed, Mars wondered. He turned onto the lane to follow Harvey and to watch him run far down the road to where someone was sitting on the ground, leaning against a fence post. So far down the lane Mars could barely make out the figure, its small frame melded into the post. When Harvey reached the person and circled around it, the person made a slight move but didn't get up. Harvey raced back to Mars, dancing around him whimpering as though to say, *Come*. Then the dog was off down the lane again to the person. Mars followed. He began to see that it could be a woman. If so, why was she sitting there? His farm stretched for a few miles in that direction and normally people didn't come around. He walked up to Emma—no one he knew. She looked up at him and squinted into a weak, frightened smile.

"Hello," Mars said.

Harvey frisked about wanting to know Emma, waiting for her to state her purpose, giving her the opportunity to show her love for a dog such as he.

"Where am I?" Emma asked. Her eyes were weak tunnels through which her life was draining out.

"You're at Wickenbird Farm. How did you get here?" The farm was too far off the paths for normal hiking. He knew before he heard her answer that she was in trouble.

"I walked. I don't know where I came from." She needed extra seconds in which to breathe. "I found myself in the woods. I think I've walked two days, maybe three, looking for something familiar." Should she fear Mars? He looked kind; it was her belief that the villagers were kindly disposed. Even so, her world had flipped some kind of turnabout leaving her out of place. "I'm so thirsty." While she spoke, she petted Harvey who had set his tail to wagging, and had rested his head on her knee.

"Well, come to the house. There's plenty of water there. You look like you need a meal and a good rest. We'll try to find out where you belong." Mars didn't question the universe much. He believed that although there might be detours along the way, most things and events sense their ultimate direction and were headed there.

"I also have a frightful headache, and there's a large lump on my head. Don't know how I got that." She touched her head.

Mars leaned over to examine the place she had touched. "I say, you've taken a blow. Your scalp is matted with blood, your eye is swollen and purple, and that's a ghastly bruise on your face." He helped Emma up, took her arm to steady her, and turned toward the farm.

She felt reassured and even possibly secure. She felt his strength and for now, that was enough, although she couldn't remember anything past two or three days ago when she started walking out of the field of bluebells. What was in store for her at the farm? What if this man asks her name?

"I am Mars Marsden, and Mum and my sister, Hannah, and I own this farm. Our buildings are down the road there." He gestured in the direction to which they were headed. Harvey kept close to Emma as the three of them walked slowly down the lane.

Emma didn't reply. She wondered whether her legs could carry her—those buildings appeared to be in another country.

"Might I ask your name?" Mars said.

The fields about hummed the only sound as Mars waited. He looked at Emma and saw her forehead wedge into a frown. Was that her headache, or did she not want to reveal her name? He could see that despite her facial swelling and bruising, she was quite pretty and definitely not a vagrant type. Surely, Hannah would help her clean up; wash the matting out of her hair.

"I can't remember my name. I know that sounds awful. I'm so tired and thirsty, and my head hurts so. Throbs. I can't think of anything right now. Perhaps when I have water, and let my brain cool, I'll remember my name." It was frightening to realize she couldn't name herself. Certainly, this man would be wondering. "There's no identity in this waist pack," she added.

When they reached the farmhouse, going in the closer, front way, Mars held open the door and waited for Emma to enter. Even Harvey waited, although normally he would have burst in happy to greet whomever he saw, knowing he or she had been breathlessly waiting for him. This time he followed Emma in, aware that this unusual situation required respectful restraint. They stepped down a hallway, and into the kitchen where a slightly stocky, reassuring, woman with a scarf tying back her hair, stood at a table kneading bread. She looked up and registered her surprise to see Emma.

"Hannah, we have a visitor," Mars said.

Hannah wiped her hands and stepped over to welcome the stranger, but before Emma could take her hand, she collapsed. Harvey whimpered, licked her cheek as though he understood that she needed to be revived. Together Hannah and Mars pulled Emma up and walked her over to a corner of the kitchen, lowering her into a chair that stood aside a fireplace. Mars pointed out to Hannah the dried blood on Emma's head.

Emma barely opened her eyes. "Hello," she whispered, the word limp as a rag.

"She was leaning against the fence about a half mile down the road," Mars said. "It was Harvey who found her. I don't know who she is, and she can't remember her name or how she got here, just that she thinks she's been walking for days. She needs water right away."

He hardly said the words before Willa, one of the farmhands, had water up to Emma's mouth, encouraging her to drink slowly. Then with a sigh, Emma lay back and closed her eyes. She was at the mercy of these people. Whatever they had in mind had to be okay, for she couldn't resist. They seemed to be kind; she felt slightly safe.

"Let's wait until she recovers some," Mars said, "then perhaps she can tell us where she belongs. Something beastly has happened to her."

A voice called from upstairs.

"I'll be right there, Mum," Hannah said.

"Go on up," Mars said. "I'll help our guest."

"I imagine she's starved, as well," Hannah said. "Let me see what Mum wants. Sara and the lads should be here any minute, and Willa has already made biscuits."

"Ah, yes. The wonderful aroma greeted us at the door."

Hannah placed the dough in a bowl, covered it with a towel, and set it in a warm corner to rise, then she went upstairs and down a long hall and into the room where her mother, Maida, waited. Mars had already started Maida's fire, and she sat before it, covered with a light throw, enjoying the delicate sun that seeking warmth, had invited itself in through curtains that billowed about an open window nearby. She turned to look at Hannah coming into the room and reached out her hand, which Hannah, taking a seat next to her, grasped. Hannah always admired the way Maida coiled her long, shining, dark hair up into a rope. Still a slender woman with a pretty face, life had thrown Maida a disappointment that she had caught with a smile.

"Good morning, Mum. I'll bring up your tray shortly. Meanwhile, what can I do for you?"

"I smell biscuits," Maida said.

"Willa has already made them, and has started our coffee, and is beginning to lay the table. Sara and the men should be here any minute, and you know how fast Sara is in the kitchen." Hannah reached behind Maida to plump her pillow. "We've had a bit of commotion down in the kitchen. Mars and Harvey came in with a stranger. A woman. They found her far down the road. We think she's lost and perhaps in shock, and anyway, she's not well. Willa gave her water, and now she's resting. She appears to have been through quite an ordeal. She has a blow to her head and a fierce bruise aside her face. But I feel certain that she's not a vagrant. Mars and I have made a doctor's appointment for her tomorrow in Wethermere."

Maida's eyes had grown wider with each of Hannah's announcements. "Indeed, I thought I heard unusual commotion below stairs. I wonder what has happened to her? Well, offer her some of Sara's good breakfast."

"Indeed, we will, Mum. We'll be at it as soon as breakfast is ready; I'll fix a tray for her and see whether she can take something. I hear the cart now; I'll go down and help. You'll be eating soon."

"Well let me know how our guest gets on, and who she is." Maida looked proudly on Hannah's face. Mars and Hannah were her grown children, and for whom to be quite proud. So proud. What good fortune she had had. She didn't know the number of years left to her, but knew they would be the best possible with Hannah's and Mars' care. And, although she was slightly crippled, she didn't want them to have the burden of her, and except for cooking and laundry, she took complete responsibility for herself. She wanted Hannah and Mars to be out and about finding mates for themselves. She had said to them several times, they could bring them here to live; this large old house could hold many more. They had friends to join for festivals and hoedowns at the community center, but so far there had been no one for them to marry, bring home, add to the family.

Soon Hannah came upstairs with a tray on which was a pot of steaming, fragrant coffee. She set the tray on a table by the window where Maida sat to watch the sun go about its business lifting the distant mist. These days, due to the great effort to negotiate the stairs, Maida didn't go down often, for she had to have help. However, she went down every Sunday and sat with her family, unwilling to give up on those pleasures. And sometimes she went with the family to Evensong in Wethermere. She loved the downstairs with its low ceilings, those heavy rafters, and in-season flowers and grasses coloring the world outside of every window. Plenty of other times Mars or Hannah would ask her to come down, they were happy to help, didn't think of it as a burden, but she didn't want to be a bother. Besides, except in the hottest weather, they kept a fire going in her bedroom. Many times Hannah and Mars had begged her to let them set up a bedroom for her in one of the many downstairs rooms. But Maida had spent her adult life with Horace in their upper front room looking out over their drive lined with lilacs and forsythias, and if the children (they were always her children) didn't mind, she hoped to stay there as long as she could. Forever, she said under her breath. Despite her life's challenge, there had been provided a "glass of blessings," a perfect crystal which she could hold up to the light and see Horace and Mars and Hannah reflected in its facets.

"Our visitor has recovered some, Mum," Hannah said. "She was so anxious to have water; I was afraid she was about to drown in it."

"Willa came up to tell me about her. She said she was right spent, and just a waif. She must have been walking and not eating for days," Maida said in between bites of biscuit.

"While you eat, Mum, I'll go down again to see if they need help."

AT SIX O'CLOCK SHARP every morning except Sunday, Sara, the Marsden's cook, arrived along with farmhands, Sol and Matt. By then, Willa had already arrived on her bicycle. They would hang their hats and coats on pegs in the mudroom behind the kitchen hallway. Sara would find a crisp white apron in the back closet, tie it around her ample waist, and go into the kitchen, eager to start the day and to start breakfast. She had worked for the Marsdens for ten happy years, knew their habits and how to cook their meals, and wouldn't work for another family, could she help it. The Marsdens; the farmhands, Sol, Matt and Willa, and her own daughter, Jane, were family. By now, Sara knew every nook and cupboard in that ancient, huge kitchen, had polished them many times, and with Willa's help, could create savory dishes for twenty people if she had to. Sol and Matt would follow her in, ready to set about starting fires throughout the drafty old farmhouse.

This morning their faces formed questions when they saw Emma sitting in the corner. Sara and the men stood uncomfortably, not knowing what to say to the strange woman who was slowly eating a biscuit dripping with honey, or whether to say anything. Waiting for an introduction from Mars, they turned questioning faces to him. He looked just as puzzled as they felt.

Mars wondered what to say about Emma. For the moment, she had no name. He wanted to say something about her, but didn't want to say it in front of her. He had to say something, though. "Our guest has perhaps wandered away from an accident, and I think she's having a mild shock."

To help warm her damp and chilled clothing, Mars had found a throw for Emma that she kept tightly snugged around her. She tried to be alert as she looked at the strangers.

"She said she has a headache and there's an obvious knot on her head. Harvey and I found her down the lane; near on to where Drips-Over meets Warbler's End."

As she took in the new arrivals Emma uttered a weak hello, but she had no energy to rouse herself.

"Well, we'll make you comfortable, Miss," Sara said nodding reassurances. She had recovered from her surprise on seeing the unexpected visitor, and resolving to treat the situation like an everyday occurrence, set about organizing the kitchen for breakfast. Whatever was to happen, people had to eat. "Scurry about, gentlemen," she said with her smiling, encouraging face. "There's much to do; you know that better than I. This old house has quite a chill on her, we need our fires a going."

Matt and Sol broke their stare, reached for wood-carriers, went out, and returned with loads of wood. Sol stoked the fire near Emma, while Matt went to build fires in other downstairs rooms. Except in hot weather it was their custom to have two or three downstairs fires going until bedtime, the old stone house could be chilly and the stones themselves seemed to welcome the added warmth. And once a month or so, Sol and Matt would take the truck to woods where they were welcomed to take fallen branches.

While they were busy building fires, Sara started breakfast; those were many mouths to feed three and sometimes four meals a day. Sara and Jane, lived on their own small farm, *Top of the Wold*, two miles down a side road. Mornings, Jane went to high school in Wethermere, riding the school bus, and Sol picked Sara up in the golf cart. He also drove her home nights. In winter, he had covers to enclose the cart and they were snug as they rode. They enjoyed meeting each other this way and at meals. Sometimes Sara took carefully prepared and tempting lunches to the men as they pruned through the orchards or mended fences, and although she had good and proper help in the kitchen from Willa, often on Saturdays, Jane came to help as well. Now Sara worked at the stove while Hannah finished setting the table.

Emma had dozed, her exhaustion nearly complete, but with the energetic movement of logs and feet thumping about, she woke. She looked around and for a moment couldn't remember where she was, or why. Then Mars came in with Harvey and looked to see how she was recovering. He looked at her kindly, and she began to remember—remember where they had found her—Mars and the dog—Harvey, Mars had called him. Harvey came over to check on her, putting his chin on her knee, offering her encouragement. She felt comfortable, and for the first time in ages, she was warm.

"I think our guest recovers some, Sara," he said. "Perhaps she can take breakfast."

"And I'm fixing a plate for her this minute."

Mars thought Emma had lost her frightened look; had, he thought, relaxed her mind some, and warmed her body, dried out her damp clothing. Soon, Sara set a tray of eggs and sausages on a table by Emma. "You can eat right here, Miss," Sara said. "No need for you to try to come to table."

Emma pulled herself up squarely. She was starving for eggs, which she could smell, and for the hot coffee that Sara set down by her.

"Enjoy it, Miss, there's more where that comes from. One thing we have plenty of around here is food. Good food and patience. You take your time, I've many chores to do here, and I'll be right handy."

Emma wanted to grab the plate of fragrant, nourishing food with her hands and heave it down in one gulp, but instead, she picked up another biscuit; homemade and generously buttered, and with honey so fresh it had to have come straight from the hive that day. So good, she could live just on that, she thought. Then she picked up a spoon, not trusting her shaky hand with the fork, and began to eat eggs. Comfort food. Never before had it meant so much. And coffee! It seemed to have been a lifetime that she had existed in the raw chill without coffee. Her damp clothes had warmed now, the fireplace was warming the entire kitchen, and cheer was finding a small place to enter Emma's soul, promising that everything would be okay. She looked like a disheveled waif, a true homeless person, hair knotted up into twists, face black and blue; hard to tell whether from dirt or from a hammering.

She looks to have taken a thorough beating, Hannah thought. She took another tray from a cupboard and laid over it a blue cloth. Then she ladled eggs and bacon onto a fine china plate.

Emma watched, trying to eat more slowly than her will desired, and trying to think who were these people, and how had she suddenly been set down among them. She had been seeking help, but hadn't expected to find such unqualified help. And she had been so chilled that she thought she could sit right in the fire, like *The Cremation of Sam McGee*. Could she sit before this fire for the rest of her days? As it was, she didn't know where else to go.

Hannah picked up the tray, now filled with all kinds of breakfast delights, and turned toward the stairs. "This is for Mum. She's not easy to work the stairs, but she does get down now and then. You'll meet her, when you're strong enough to go up; she's always looking for company, and farmers just don't drop in often enough—too busy. So Mum is eager to meet you." Hannah's smile was welcoming.

With fireplaces now warming throughout the house, Sol and Matt sat at the table and waited while Sara and Willa placed heaping platters of food down the table's length. Willa poured coffee around—six cups—then from a warming oven, she took baskets of biscuits which she placed in the middle of the table. Now Mars joined them. From where he sat, he could keep an eye on Emma. Hannah came downstairs, took her seat, and started passing baskets and platters down the table. Eager hands reached at once for a biscuit.

"Aye, Willa, we know your biscuits, and we aren't waiting long for one," Sol said.

Sara and Willa took their seats and a mumble of grace circled the hungry friends. Mars tucked in a plea for the Lord to help their guest. *Amen* lofted from six voices, and serious eating began. Each knew that two of the pleasures of working at the Marsden's farm were good food, and the companionship of eating together.

"Miss," Mars said looking over at Emma, "you're welcome to join us at table, but we think you need your rest and warmth right where you are. Please excuse all us hungry farmers eating without you. We've much work ahead of us that we have to get to. Farm work never stops, seldom takes a day off."

Emma gave him a weak smile.

While they ate, each heart and each mind was thinking about Emma. Who was this woman cast suddenly among them? Each wanted to stare at her, something appealing about her. Was it her matted hair that curled up so with the humidity? Her gamine appearance? Or was it her seeming frangibleness? Each one of them wanted to come to her aid. They didn't stare, but Mars mainly had to work at stilling his eyes, keeping them on his plate. He had only begun to have a minute really to see her. And there were those questions to himself: what had happened to her? What had she been through? Something had struck a couple nasty whacks to her head and face. Was she still in danger from someone?

Willa rose and carried the coffee pot over to Emma; she did indeed look ready for a refill. Emma sipped at it, grateful for the stimulation, feeling the warmth, facing her fears head on. What was next? What could she do next? Go where? It felt like days that she had labored under this confusion. These people seemed gentle, even kind, and she was at their mercy, but how long would they cater to her? What could show her where she belonged?

X

The Marsdens of Wickenbird Farm

Maida was able to take care of herself just fine, it was just that she couldn't walk far, or do the stairs easily, nor could she stand long enough for such activities as cooking. Her crippled state had been slowly coming on now for fifty years, her heart growing weaker with each passing year. When she was a child on a visit with her mother to a poor family, they had carried in a basket of homemade bread and other food items, and then Maida and the child of the family had romped out back, passed the garden, into a pile of discarded household stuff. There Maida had leaped over a rusty iron bed frame, ripping across her knee in the process. She hadn't been worried about the small cut and had continued to play. Later, when her mother called her to leave and saw the cut, she took her inside and washed and wrapped her knee. Still there was just enough time for staph to take hold, to stiffen her knee permanently, and to weaken her heart.

By the time the extent of her illness became evident, the doctors said it was too late to reverse the damage, and in ensuing years, her knee would not bend at all, and her heart had become weak enough to prevent most activities. The good fortune was that her parents could leave to her the farm and enough financial resources so that she could hire the necessary farmhands and household help for cooking and cleaning.

She had met Horace at a community festival and although everyone in the county knew of her affliction, and thought she probably could not have children, in time, and not a long time at all, Horace had found the great amount of love for her necessary to ask her to marry him. He wanted her for his wife. He didn't have to have children; he had to have her. For him, in no other face ever again, would he see a woman with whom he wanted to share his life. But I may not live forever, she had said looking up to him with her soft laugh. She wanted to say *might not live long at all*, but she couldn't put such a bad spin on things. I'll take my chances he had said.

Two years later Hannah was born and two years after that came Mars. The night Mars arrived, Horace had been viewing the sky with his telescope, in particular looking for the planet, Mars. When he found it, he called out, *I found Mars*! That was the very second the midwife called out the upstairs window to him that the baby was a boy. Horace figured the boy had truly earned his name. Unlike the red planet's warring reputation, the boy, Mars, was as gentle as the smallest pup.

Horace tended his family with care and love and when he had a dogcart turn over on him on his way to market, and end his life, his small family didn't see how they could go on without him. But as they must, as they had to, they gradually began to fill the place Horace had left; gradually learned, though he was not ever out of their hearts, to live their days without him. At that time Hannah was twelve and Mars ten, and for some time they had helped with chores; for some time had put in a good day's work and studied their lessons. They grew strong and even wise. By day, they rode their horses to the schoolhouse, and at night by the fire, they studied history, grammar, and math. Gradually as they grew, and as Maida weakened, Hannah and Mars found themselves running the farm, caring for the buildings, sheep, cows, chickens, geese, orchards, and gardens. They had grown in wisdom and knowledge for all the farm's requirements. And they had friends to join for events at the community center in Wethermere. Though Wickenbird Farm was isolated, its occupants were not.

Needing additional occupation for the long winter days, Mars had worked up a side business caning chairs. He reworked wicker from old furniture he found in second-hand stores. He had a collection of nice old, or antique, chairs ready for caning, and had turned one of the farm's buildings that he heated with a wood-burning stove, into a small studio. Winter days, when farm requirements were slow, he was often there either caning, or soaking willow reeds. Then, in spring, he would sell a chair or two at the market, and occasionally, when he had a few on hand that were finished, he would run a notice in the local newspaper. He could turn a broken throwaway into a jewel. People came round to buy, for he had developed a reputation that had spread throughout the county.

Then Emma stumbled down their road, and into their lives.

"What is she to do?" Mars asked Hannah. They were on a walk to cut forsythia for the house.

"I can't imagine, but certainly she can stay here until she knows. She's not a burden . . . always trying to help."

Two days had passed since Mars and Harvey had found Emma, and Hannah had freshened one of the unused bedrooms and had urged Emma to feel comfortable there. Be right at home. With that strong force showing in her eyes, you didn't have to know Hannah more than five minutes to understand the strength of her intent.

"She still doesn't know her name," Mars said, "let alone where she came from, or how she happened to spring up on our road, but her strength is improving. It was a relief to get Dr. Turnrod's opinion that her concussion was minor and he didn't expect continued problems."

Deeply concerned about the lump on Emma's head and bruising on her face and eye, Mars and Hannah had taken her to their doctor in Wethermere. Explanations were tricky—their not knowing how to explain to the doctor Emma's arrival—but when he came into the examining room, Emma saved the moment by stepping right up to tell him that she had walked away from something, she knew not what, and had amnesia, and the

Marsdens had found her, helped her, had taken her in. Mars and Hannah didn't have to say anything. Dr. Turnrod had confirmed their assumptions that she had indeed been struck hard several times, once to the back of her head, and several times to the side. He explained that Emma seemed to have retrograde amnesia: she could remember everything after a certain event, and nothing before. He had recommended that ice packs be applied to the swelling—which treatment they said they had already started.

"Yes. And he expected that in time she would recover her memory. . . probably soon," Hannah said.

"She's quite pleasant, actually. Nice to have around," Mars said. He found that he looked forward to Emma's smile. For a long time, he had been much too full of work to look about at smiles; had any been near other than his family's, and those were family kinds of smiles. Emma's was something apart—a magnetic pull for him.

"And Mum loves her." Hannah caught the glint in Mars' eye that said he found Emma to be special, as well.

Back in the house, as Mars arranged the forsythia in a vase, he looked over at Emma, who while mending a tablecloth, had been listening to Sara telling her all about the farm. Emma had recovered much of her strength, and had asked for something to do to help. "Idle hands are the devil's workshop," she said to Mars. She laughed. "See, I can remember silly aphorisms. Some part of my brain is functioning."

"And a good part," he said. "The other parts will pay jealous attention, and come on line shortly." He searched for what to call her. "We don't know what to call you," he said. "We don't want to keep calling you Miss."

"I have an idea," Sara said. "Jane's art teacher has had the class look for found items, odd things, natural things, and they're called, 'objet trouvé'. Trouvé is a pretty sound for a pretty woman. Until we know better, let's call you Trouvé. If you don't mind, of course."

"Perfect," said Mars. "Although you're not an object, you were certainly found, and Harvey and I found you!" He looked at Emma and laughed. She seemed pleased with this outcome, pleased that it was Mars who had found her. She was acquainted with objet trouvé, and didn't mind being one. Quite amusing to her in fact.

And thus it was that Emma became Trouvé.

"Has there been any news at all about a missing woman?" Maida asked. It was teatime, and Emma had come up with the tray, followed by Hannah and Mars. A soft mauve light joined in, working its way through the closed window, closed against the outside chill. It was the middle of March now; evenings could still be raw, and Maida had that beautiful rose-colored afghan spread over her lap, the one Hannah had made for her. She sat by the fire that Matt kept going throughout the day and evening. Now and then Maida gave Harvey a pat; he preferred to make himself comfortable next to her chair, knowing he would get attention.

"No Mum," Mars said. "Most mysterious."

He spoke over Emma's head, but Emma was used to it; used to the puzzle about her origin, where she was meant to be. And she knew she was welcome at Wickenbird Farm. Indeed, they already loved her, and she them. But then, she knew they were people quick to love.

"Neither the telly nor the papers, nor Constable Jones report a missing woman. You just dropped down from the sky," Mars said. "To our good fortune."

Emma had begun to spend an hour or so each day with Maida, either reading or playing word games to help Emma's memory, but today Mars said he would like to take Trouvé to the farmers' market in the village of Cav Neumont. It was that time of year when he and Matt would load the truck with spring produce and bundles of flowers, and perhaps a chair—and park at the market. They would be there all day, he said, and Trouvé might like to help; might like a change. Maybe she would recognize something or someone. Emma, now known to the Marsdens as 'Trouvé', had no idea whether she had been to Cav Neumont.

Maida said, "Do go, Trouvé, I think you'll enjoy it. Mars, take her and Matt to supper afterward at the Bucket. Matt's such a good lad and works so hard."

"A bonnie idea," said Mars, his head nodding, his face filled with a smile.

Emma looked up at him, questioning; she had been reading to Maida. Going to the market did seem like a splendid idea but for the fear always lurking just beneath her thoughts. Would it be worse to face that unknown? If she could stay close to Mars, she should be safe. How to say that without sounding juvenile?

"Yes, Trouvé, it will be a fine thing we'll do. We'll take supper at the Bucket Arms. I think you could use a treat and I want to treat you." He wished he could remove the fear he read across her brow; he yearned to use his hand to smooth it away. "You'll see; the villagers are more eccentric than we Marsdens . . . a great study. And the market's so colorful . . . so much to see. It's famous. People come to it from all over the county."

At 7.00 a.m. the next morning, while Sara packed lunches for them to take, Mars, Matt, and Emma loaded the white truck with bushels of peas, lettuce, spinach, and flowers that sat just outside the mudroom door. Everything had to be layered in carefully, just like working a puzzle.

Fully loaded, the truck rumbled slowly along oiled dirt roads, taking its time as though it knew flowers were patiently passing the time in back, standing in pails of water, lightly covered against the breeze. Then when the truck reached pavement, it seemed to take its head, and proudly made good time. They mostly rode in silence, Emma dazed by the rolling fields—new ones, those she hadn't seen before; Mars dazed by Emma, her scent better than the lavender that he often cut for the house. The truck held the road so quietly that with windows down to catch the aromas of the spring-green fields, they could hear occasional birdsongs. Emma wore a soft blue dress that two days back, Hannah had found for her among her own dresses. Hannah said she hoped Trouvé didn't mind wearing someone else's clothing, but maybe it would do—they got to a dress shop so seldom. It had had to be belted up at the waist, as Hannah was a size larger than Emma. But that was fine—Emma said it fitted perfectly and was lovely. The dress's pale blue background had tiny pumpkin-colored spots, and softly draped around Emma in a perfect manner. "I'm lucky that it fits," Emma said. "I'll wear it proudly." So, Emma had exactly one dress, and one pair of jeans—the ones in which she had arrived—and one pair of hiking shoes. Today her jeans were in the wash.

Riding along in the truck Emma daydreamed, recalling her strange night dreams in which indistinct images of special people would appear. Sometimes she could almost see a young man and she would wonder who he was and call to him, but the image was never clear and wouldn't last but a few seconds. In a few dreams, she could see herself eating with people in a grand house. Who were they? Where was that? Sometimes she saw herself hiking; that dream always ended in terror. Why was that?

Mars had found a new shyness in himself around Emma. Her soft manner invited his caring and a desire to protect her. He found that he couldn't impose on her too much of his attention; had to respect that she must feel trapped. Now he wanted to glance at her as she rode along beside him in the truck. He wanted to say something, but nothing of import would come to him—just gibberish. And he didn't want to fill this precious time with gibberish.

When they reached the village row of shops, Mars slowed before a store and said, "There's a dress shop just there, but it won't open for several hours. I'll try to set up the truck in a spot where you can see it from that shop, then you can walk across and buy yourself a dress. You must be tired of Hannah's and tired of your jeans by now."

"But Mars, I have no money."

"I have money," he said. And with a twinkle, "I have wads of money."

"But I don't want to spend yours."

"Don't worry, Trouvé, I understand. You'll earn it. Every penny."

He drove to the end of the block and swung around the corner into the market area. While villagers and tourists were milling about waiting, eager to buy, farmers and vendors were organizing trucks and stalls, almost ready to open the market. Brightly colored banners waved about announcing important opportunities. Soon shoppers were stopping by Mars' truck looking and buying. The Marsden's produce and flowers had that just-picked look, for indeed they had been; there was none to be found fresher, and it wasn't long—watching and listening to Mars and Matt—until Emma learned what to say, and how to price. And she found that indeed, her help was needed with wrapping. Genuine help. She felt good about that, for they were rushed with buyers waiting in line.

At the time for the dress shop to open, Mars handed Emma a wad of bills and urged her to go ahead and shop; buy the clothes she needed. "You can easily see our truck from over there. We'll quit at about 5:00 p.m. for that supper we're going to have at the Bucket. Even though Sara packed lunches for us, we'll be ravenously hungry by then."

Emma clutched the bills; she had no purse, but she found that Hannah's dress had a pocket, and she folded the bills into it, then she crossed over to the dress shop. As she crossed, she looked up and down the street, straining to remember something, anything; see something familiar, something to connect her to her own history. But aside from a few vague feelings of familiarity, nothing called out to her *you know me*. When she entered the shop, she couldn't say why, but she knew exactly on which side the dresses hung, and on which side hung slacks, and she knew she would find jeans folded along the center aisle, and robes and gowns hanging in back. She felt the need to examine every corner for a threat just waiting to lunge at her, but no one was in the store except for the clerk. Emma pushed down her fear and turned toward the dresses. When the sales clerk gave Emma a bright hello, Emma responded, hoping for recognition, looking at the clerk with the question—do we know each other? But she sensed no familiarity in the clerk, who straight away turned to arrange merchandise. Emma began to thumb through dresses. Size?

"What size do you think I wear?" she asked the clerk.

Organizing her face into doubt, the clerk turned to Emma and asked, "Don't you wear an eight?" Strange, she thought, a woman who doesn't know her size.

Emma said, "Thank you," and moved forward across the rack toward the eights. "Your dresses are lovely," she said, "and I'll take this one." She pulled out a pale-yellow knee-length dress. "I believe this is percale," she said. *How did she know that*? "The silk next to it is quite fine, and lovely, but I would have limited use for it on the farm." She managed an insecure laugh. "This percale will be perfect. And washable." Emma looked around not sure what to do next.

"You can use the little room in the back for fitting," the clerk said.

"No. There's no need to try it. I know it will fit perfectly, and I haven't much time. We have a stall across at the market."

The clerk took the dress, removed the hanger, and carefully folded the dress into a box lined with tissue paper. Then she added pairs of jeans and underwear that Emma had handed to her. She thought Emma appeared rather vague, in some respect—lost, and she had no purse with her either. Odd. For a flicker of a second thinner than a hair's breadth, the clerk wondered whether she had seen the woman before, a while back. However, she didn't remember a woman who lived on a farm.

"Did you say you lived on a farm?"

"Yes. Not in this county though," Emma said. She must protect herself from something, though she had no idea what it was. "Far from here—we're just in for the market."

Then Emma tried on shoes. She needed a soft pair for the house; give her hiking shoes a rest. Then she chose a wide-brimmed hat to shield against any sun that might challenge the weather, and she asked the clerk to remove its tag so she could wear it. She loved the hat and with it on she felt more like the farmer she would try to be, or at least pretend to be while helping at the market. The clerk placed the shoes into a box and then into a bag. Emma held out her bills and the clerk selected a few, rang up the sale, and handed Emma change. The clerk wanted to do something special for this woman who seemed a bit unsure of herself somehow, and she reached under the counter, cut away a long length of yellow-silk ribbon, tied it around the dress box, fashioned a large bow, and placed the box in the bag with the shoes.

"That's lovely," Emma said. "Thank you kindly."

The sales clerk held the door for her, and as she did so, she stared hard at Emma, about to ask, *were you in here last year*? But Emma hurried so, eager to get back to Mars and safety, that the clerk had no chance to.

Emma crossed over to Mars' truck, easy to spot with its profusion of orchid and yellow spring blooms, even on the bonnet and roof of its cab where Mars had placed baskets of dried flowers and pails of fresh ones in water. He hadn't missed a color, she thought, purple, even white. It must be the most colorful spot at the market. She looked forward to the rest of the day helping Mars: this man, who was always so kind and patient with her in her confusion. As well, she delighted in the variety of customers who bought from him.

Many shoppers knew from previous years that this truck was where they would find the finest lettuce and spinach, fresh out of the ground; picked just this morning. Strawberries sweet as honey. And honey. Tourists and villagers were sauntering along looking—a day's outing. A fine day for everyone. Breaking puffy clouds moved about letting in just enough sun, as though protecting the denizens below from too many of its rays. A breeze touched down as though to see what went on. And supper at the Bucket Arms. Had she been there? Why was that strange name familiar?

"I didn't know who you were when you walked up," Mars said, "with your new hat shielding your face so, and your hair tucked under. It took me a second or two to see you were indeed our Trouvé. I'm glad you thought of a hat. One never knows how much sun we're likely to have." He turned to a customer; there was work to be done: bundling flowers, filling customer bags, taking their money, making change (this Mars or Matt took care of, for Emma worried about getting the change right), all while swapping the news of the day. It was entertainment time. For a while, everyone forgot his and her concerns and problems.

The market stretched out down a long lane with additional short avenues branching off on the sides. After they had been working for a few hours, Mars said to Emma, "Take yourself for a walk. It's slowed up a bit. Many people are taking lunch now, so Matt and I can handle the customers. You'll find your way back to the truck easily enough. Just don't leave the market area. Should you get disoriented, probably almost anyone can point you to our truck." He worried about her slightly, but she seemed to be grounded enough not to get lost. "You might enjoy seeing all the stalls."

She did want to walk around. She felt safer now that she had endured shopping alone. "Thank you. I will," she said, and she looked down the lane, hesitated, and started. The market seemed to have everything known under the sun—and then some. There were even racks of dresses, which she looked through, but none so fine as the one already bought and waiting back at the truck. Amusing to look through them though. There were tourist items of every description and stalls and stalls of produce; none so fine appearing as those Mars grew. She felt fortunate. Somehow, she had found these exceptional people: Mars and his family, who had taken her in when she was lost.

Just then, ahead, but at the end of a long lane, she watched a man who seemed to be unable to pull away his gaze from her. What was so appealing about his appearance, a familiar silhouette, yet too far away? Could she have known him? He was with two women, and one of the women turned for a moment to see where the man's gaze had lighted, and when she saw Emma, seemed to start and herself to stare. Emma thought the woman might wave, but then she turned back and with her arm in the man's arm, hurried him along. They moved farther away into the distance. Why did they appear to stare at her, Emma wondered. Perhaps she imagined it, easy to do with such a congestion of people gyrating about. She hurried down the lane to find out who the man and woman were; they would think she was crazy—perhaps she was. Yet, maybe they knew who she was and where she belonged. But they had disappeared in the crowd. With the feeling that she had missed an opportunity, Emma tried to forget it and continued to browse, and after turning down almost every lane, she turned back to the truck.

When it was 4:30 p.m. Mars said, "Let's close down the truck. Nothing much left anyway. It's been a good day. Our work is well done, and I'm thirsty for a pint. How about you?" His wide and warm smile wrapped around Emma.

"I'm starved," she said. "I hope they know we're coming and have a bountiful menu. It's been all I could do not eating all your peas, raw, shell and all, and some of the hay you have under the baskets." She laughed.

"I thought you sounded more like a horse every hour. I was tempted to hang a feed bucket around your neck." He loved her laugh, and wanted every opportunity to inspire it. As well, he loved her face and had to work to keep his eyes off it. Perhaps he loved *her*. "Let's leave the truck here and walk across. It'll be fine here. I made a reservation for us at 5:00 p.m. just in case."

At the Bucket Arms Mars ordered three ice-cold ales for them while they studied the menu. "I could eat everything on here at once," he said. "How about you, Trouvé?" And he gave Emma an expectant, questioning nod. "I'm treating you Matt, for your tireless work today. And every day, I might add. You won't have to spend your earnings. Order exactly what you want. The farm is having a good year."

He's kind, Emma thought, truly kind. When she looked up at Mars and smiled her appreciation, she had to work against that mysterious gravity anchoring her eyes to his. Turning to the menu, she said, "I don't remember when I last saw a menu, and I want to dissect it item by item." After she had carefully studied every menu item, she said she would have the chicken pie. But her thoughts had turned to how to double her efforts to repay this family.

"A fine choice," Mars said, "but I haven't had a steak in months, and I'm eager for one, and I'll wager you are also, Matt. So, as God is my witness, Matt's head is nodding affirmatively, ready to nod itself off; we'll have the sirloin." He signaled the waiter and when he came, Mars ordered for the three of them, and added, "We're all dried out, my man. Kindly bring us three more ales." After the waiter left to place their order, Mars said, "It hasn't been long that our pubs have served dinners. You must know that. But this pub, which is rather large, as taverns go, has always been counted on for respectable fare. Before she became more handicapped, I used to bring Mum here for a meal now and then. Get her out of the hot kitchen; she loved to cook and was usually at work in the kitchen."

"I'm sure, on some level, your mother misses that," Emma said. "However, she seems quite happy with her life. I believe I have a kitchen somewhere. I think I have made bread. I watched Sara kneading and knew the feel of it and exactly what to do next."

"Do you recall being in a pub?"

"I do. I know I have. I just don't remember specifics." She looked around the tavern at the soft woods and colorful lights—just bright enough to illuminate the warm ambiance that invited customers. "I noticed when we came in that there were many buckets behind the bar, hanging up over the bartender's head," Emma said. "What are they for?"

"In ancient times, women were not allowed to come into the tavern. However, they could bring a bucket to a window and the waiter or bartender would fill it with stew. Sometimes a woman would arrive at the window without a bucket, hoping the tavern would lend her one. As it was such a popular tavern, this occurred all too often, thus the owner was constrained to keep a supply of buckets. and eventually that settled down into the current name, The Bucket Arms. There's always a story around the naming of our pubs and inns, sometimes a long story, often lost to memory."

As they took their leisurely supper, they talked about the successful day. They had sold out—nearly everything gone from that loaded truck. "It's a good thing we don't need to work the market again tomorrow," Mars said. "For I want to take Harvey to the vet—there's one in Chipping Campden—have his bum leg examined. You might like to go with me, Trouvé, see another village. Mum can do without you for another day. We mustn't let her get too spoiled with all your attention and reading."

"It's my pleasure," Emma said. "In every way I can, I want to repay your kindness for helping me, and also, I want to see Chipping Campden, it sounds familiar."

The longer Emma looked around the pub, the more familiar it seemed, but the puzzling sense of familiarity would wave in, and then be gone before she could hold on to it. The effort to remember made her dizzy. "I feel I know this place. I sense, for example that the room swings leftward into an el down there at the back. And on the right, that table in the rear . . .." But she said no more. She stared toward the back of the room, but the memory sat right on the edge in a shadow and would not budge.

Then the image formed of the man she had seen down the lane with the woman who had stared at her—nearly ready to wave, Emma thought, but who instead took the man's arm and hustled him farther away. "I thought I saw familiar people today," Emma said. "But they were so far off. A man with two women. I think they stared at me, but didn't wave and then they turned away and went on. Too quick and too far away. Yet, I felt they were familiar. I guess it doesn't matter. I did go after them but they quickly disappeared into the crowd."

"I don't believe you are from these parts," Mars said, looking at her with his serious face. "No one appears to recognize you. We could ask, but I noticed that the bartender, whom we passed on our way in, showed no recognition, nor does our waiter. Perhaps if we came another day when there's a shift change. Of course, it would help could we but know which town you came from," Mars said. "Does this one seem familiar?"

"Occasionally I'll see something that triggers a memory trying to break through. Or it could be the sound of something, or a scent. And then it fails."

"And as we've all said many times, your accent is not from England. I doubt this is where you belong. I found you at Wickenbird, far from here."

"It felt as though I had walked for two or three days. I guess I was always going in the wrong direction, wherever that was. And, as you know, when you found me, I was at the complete end of my strength. I could see your buildings down the road, but didn't think I could get there. I had passed two other houses but no one would come to the door."

"Probably all out in the field," Mars said.

Trouvé looked happy, he thought. Bringing her to the market was a splendid idea. And her new hat—fetching the way she had it angled just so.

"Your hat is right smart and it has the added function of shielding your bruises a bit. Or else, Trouvé, people might expect that I've beaten you."

"Oh, if anyone asks," Matt said, "I'll tell them that you whip all your help to keep them in line." And Matt flung out a backhand by way of example, "Whop!"

"Classic," Mars said. And he felt Trouvé's smile at Matt's antics wash over them like honey over biscuits.

Just at the moment when Mars was asking Emma how she had slept on the trail—and at the same moment when she was leaning closer to hear him over the din—daylight shone through the open entry as a man and two women came in. The waiter made a great effort for the new arrivals, bowing and all, then showed them to the rear of the room where the party disappeared around to the left. Lord Haversham had just come in with Lady Mardling and Brenda. With Emma's back to the entry, she had not seen them, and over Mars' question, it took a second for his lordship's voice to register with Emma, and by the time she turned to the familiar sound, the people were around the corner out of sight.

That voice—why did it cause her anguish? She couldn't see where they were seated. Perhaps around the corner? Could she but slip around the corner and look. There was good reason to, but she didn't have enough information, and it would be awkward. And she wasn't sure now what she had heard. Certain names such as Cav Neumont and Bucket Arms meant something to her, but she could not bring forth a meaning. It felt much like a dream that slipped into oblivion before you could mull it over.

Had Emma been seated but one table more toward the rear she might have seen through the window, Lord Haversham when he parked the Bentley and ushered the two women through the parking lot toward the Bucket's front entrance.

Lord Haversham had been Pressured into taking Lady Mardling and Brenda to the market. While the women looked at displays, his lordship had lagged on the side lines, wishing he were home, but always looking for Emma.

"I *love* this painting," Brenda said, as she pulled out a framed oil. "Think they will ship it home for me?" She looked at Simon with the question. The oil was of a landscape with each foreground blossom heavily detailed, thickly paint encrusted, looking tired.

His lordship's shudder was constrained, but Lady Mardling let hers fly as she said, "Ghastly!" Her neck stiffened back in an arch enabling her to look farther down her nose. As Lord Haversham turned away, Brenda took her cue from Lady Mardling and set down the painting. And so it went: Brenda enthusing without exception, and Lady Mardling looking down her nose and uttering sparse, belittling, comments. Lord Haversham protested the fate that left him saddled for the day with two tiresome women.

For a minute, far down the lane he saw an image that looked so familiar, his heart raced. But the image wore a hat; Emma never wore a hat. Lady Mardling, following his gaze, had looked also, said it looked like a member of his staff out for a day off, admonished him for being so liberal with the staff, and whipped him around fast on down the lane.

"Maybe it's Emma," he had said.

But Lady Mardling spoke up, "Simon! She's gone! She wanted to leave—just didn't want the confrontation of saying so. In my experience Americans are unreliable. Present company excepted." She let go a quick look at Brenda, but apparently Brenda hadn't heard, had seemed more interested in pulling Simon along.

Could that have been Emma? Brenda wondered. No. Emma wasn't breathing when she left her in the bluebells. This was her nerves getting to her because Simon acted suspicious.

But while the women were looking at little ornamental boxes, his lordship had ducked around the back corner of a stall and had stood there in a shadow until Lady Mardling and Brenda looked for him, and thinking he had proceeded on, they had followed. However, he had turned back in the direction toward where he saw the woman who, he thought, resembled Emma. He quickly passed down the main corridor studying everyone, looking down all side lanes. He passed a truck covered with produce and flowers, briefly watched two men filling orders for a waiting crowd. Then disappointed that there was no Emma in sight, he reminded himself that had she been around, she would have been with him, not gone missing without a word.

If the disappointment of having to entertain the women for the day hadn't been torture enough for him, enduring Miss Evans' meal habits now piled on—what with her waving her fork about in the air as though she were a choir conductor. He dug into his salmon while half listening to the women jostle barbs about what was good at the market, and what was not, each surprised at the opinions of the other. Soon, he hoped, DCI Adams would release

Miss Evans to go back to the States, and he would assure somehow that she did so. And now as he dined with the women, he wanted only to lean on his elbows in a spiritless exhaustion, sip wine, and think about Emma. But perhaps, he thought, that was because this place was where he had seen Emma for the first time. Last fall.

When the women had finished their meal, had finished their harping, and he could be released to leave and head on home—as they were leaving the pub, he noticed that wonderful scent; he knew it was something about Emma. And yet when he looked around, she was not there.

XI

Brenda and Lady Joan

All fires were extinguished and the manor lay dark throughout. Only Schrödinger slinked about keeping watch on such things as would interest a cat. And even he would soon select a favorite chair and call it quits for the day. Only the moon shone in its regular place against the towers and on the bats that hunted for unwary insects. Lord Haversham, John Britely and all the staff had taken to sleep hours ago. Among the two-footed inhabitants of the manor, only Brenda lay awake entertaining a thought about something she had been denying herself for a few days. It seemed impossible to deny it any longer. Her thoughts pictured the small clock on Emma's bed table. She had seen it when she was there to take a few of Emma's things: comb, make-up, backpack, to show that Emma had planned to leave. The clock looked like real gold, and had the tiniest tick; she had knelt to hear it, picking it up to read its inscription: *Tempus rerum imperator*, then she had set it back in its place—better leave it. Still, afterward, she had frequently pictured the little clock, thinking how nice it would be to own. The manor had hundreds of treasures; how could a tiny clock be missed? She felt it should be hers. To her that inscription meant *imperative to run with it*.

She could find her way in the dark down to Solar. She pictured the various hallways and how far down it was to Emma's door. She could easily make those turns, and take the clock. With Emma gone, who would know? All was quiet now; no one about, she would go quickly and take it, then stow it in the bottom of her make-up case. She opened her door and quietly looked up and down the hall. She knew that John's and Peter's rooms were to her right and she would have to pass their doors, but with her soft slippers, she could do that silently, and besides, Peter was up at college. She stepped out and started down the hall. Faint moonlight shone through the stained-glass window at the end of the hall. Then, just at the end, where she knew it turned to the left, at that intersection, she thought she saw something move. She stopped and stared, felt a chill, then nothing, just her fears in the dark. She could see the colors from the window applying themselves to a mosaic creation on the waxed floor and to chests that lined the hall. She continued to the end and went left down the next hall. She wouldn't have to pass Simon's door, for Solar came up first, and when she reached Solar, she carefully turned the handle and looked in. She could see everything in the moonlighted room. She stepped in, took the clock, and quickly left the room, closing the door slowly and gently, careful not to make a sound. Then she turned back down the hall. She felt good about her daring, and good about having the clock. She had seen such treasures in display windows along Madison Avenue, but never expected to own one.

Now she reached the hallway's junction at the window where the colors played about, and she turned right, toward her room. Again, looking ahead, she thought she saw something move. This time, whatever it was, was moving closer to her—gliding actually, something white. And when she saw Lady Joan's hair waving about as Lady Joan closed in on her, the scream that Brenda let out rattled and reverberated throughout the hall in all directions. She dropped the clock and froze. She continued to scream as Lady Joan glared menacingly at her, moving closer, forcing her to keep backing up.

John Britely shot out of his bedroom.

"Help me," Brenda cried. She appeared frozen: unable to move.

Then John saw Lady Joan. In the scattered moonlight, she took on an eerie glow; excited photons electrifying her space. She seemed grounded and real, threatening, as her spirit held Brenda fixed, immobile. John relaxed. "That's our ghost, Lady Joan," he said. "We've told you about her. She must have wondered what you were doing in the hall at this hour. She's a curious ghost, and has never harmed anyone."

As John spoke Lady Joan moved directly through a wall and out of sight. Looking around to assure that Lady Joan was indeed gone, Brenda quit screaming and seemed calmer. "You can safely go to your room," John said. "Lady Joan won't cause you any trouble. She's actually a good old soul—very old." He went to Brenda's door and held it open for her. "Actually, what are you doing up and about at this hour? Do you need something? Perhaps I can help."

"N- No," Brenda stuttered, but her senses had returned. "I couldn't sleep, so I thought I would go see the colors at the end of the hall. So unusual that window in the moonlight." *Quick thinking.*

They closed their doors behind them and once more, the manor settled into the quiet night. As John lay waiting for sleep, he pictured Lady Joan and wondered why she appeared so electrified and angry. He had not before seen her like that.

Brenda lay down; her tremor from the experience was tapering off. She found it difficult to fall asleep, afraid Lady Joan would appear in the room; there was no counting on beings who didn't have to respect walls. The clock! She had dropped the clock. Well, she wasn't going back out in that hallway; she would look for it early in the morning.

But in the morning, Ellie, up early to begin her duties, found the clock. She took it to Mrs. Penrose, and they had quite a discussion over their coffee about how the little clock might have come to be there, on the floor, in the hall. They knew nothing about the night encounters of Miss Evans, Mr. Britely, and Lady Joan.

XII

The Clock

"Your Lordship, Mrs. Penrose just handed me the clock I believe you gave to Ms. Chapman."

Lord Haversham sat at breakfast scanning the newspaper and drinking coffee. He looked up in surprise, as Brooks handed him the clock.

"Mrs. Penrose said that Ellie found it early this morning on the floor in the upper south hall."

Lord Haversham studied the clock, turning it round about in amazement. His surprise was split between the question: why was it there? and the pain for Emma's leaving—her image ever before him. The clock had been his Christmas gift to Emma, and he knew she treasured it. Wouldn't leave it behind. "Ah . . . indeed, that is a mystery. Thank you, Brooks. Certainly, something abnormal afoot."

John Britely arrived for breakfast, said good morning to Lord Haversham, and stood at the sideboard to fill his plate while Brooks poured his coffee.

"Good morning, John," Lord Haversham said. "Something most unusual going on last night. This morning Ellie found this in your hallway." He held up the clock.

John turned to see what his lordship was talking about. When he saw the clock, he stopped still, balancing his plate of eggs and sausages. He stared at the clock and then at his lordship. "What? How?" He pictured the hallway scene during the night, the encounter with Miss Evans and Lady Joan.

"Indeed. Those are good questions."

"Did you hear Miss Evans' screams last night?" John asked.

"No. What happened?"

"She was walking about when Lady Joan appeared. Scared the stuffing out of her. Her screams brought me flying out of my room thinking for all the world she was under attack by an intruder. I calmed her down and after explaining that Lady Joan was harmless, I saw Miss Evans into her room."

"That woman!"

John knew his lordship referred to Miss Evans, not to their resident ghost. "She said she couldn't sleep, and had decided to walk down the hall where she knew the moonlight would be dancing about through the stained-glass window."

"And then this morning, the little clock on the floor."

"Yes, sir."

"That clock would have been on Emma's bed table, I'm certain."

John took his seat next to Lord Haversham and the two men stared at the little clock.

"*Tempus rerum imperator,*" Lord Haversham said. "Time is the commander of all things. Well, perhaps. However, I think we have a conflicting commanding problem in the manor. I'll ask Mrs. Penrose to keep the door to Solar locked, as well as the doors to certain other rooms."

They looked up to see Brenda enter. Her cheerful manner was on display as she fairly bobbed about, nodding to them a good morning. Then she turned to the sideboard, took a plate and filled it. As she did so, she thought, as she had numerous times since arriving at the manor, that this was the life for her—a fine array of food at each meal, just handed to you, no hassle about cooking, no clean-up, no pots, no pans. Whereas, her life with Luke seemed like slavery when compared. She had awakened determined to act as though walking down the hall in the middle of the night to see the moonlight was not an unusual thing to do when one couldn't sleep, and she was also determined to assure John and Simon that what *was* unusual was that horrid ghost. What would they think about the clock, she wondered. As soon as she dressed, she had walked the hall looking for it—unsuccessfully. Someone had beaten her to it. Someone must be wondering, but no one could accuse *her*.

Lord Haversham and John said nothing; kept their thoughts to themselves while they watched Brenda take her seat when Brooks held it out for her. Then Brenda saw the clock. She had begun to take a sip of coffee, but on seeing the clock almost before her place, her hand trembled as she clanked down her cup. She recovered instantly. She would show that she had never before seen that clock.

"I could absolutely not sleep last night," she said emphatically, with her cheerful face looking to the men for sympathy. "And I'm afraid I woke John when that ghastly ghost gave me such a fright. Have you seen the moonlight through that window at the end of the hall?" Her sentences were running on.

No one answered.

"It's so beautiful, you must stay up late some night and see the effect."

Still no one answered and Brenda felt the need to rant on. "Is there someplace here where I can be safe from that ghost? She's enough to scare one to death, and I'm sure my heart is weaker today than it was yesterday."

Neither his lordship nor John had a reply; they simply looked at their plates and pushed their food around as they attempted to sort things out—the clock, Brenda, the middle of the night.

"My deepest apologies, John. I hope you were able to go back to sleep." Brenda looked at Simon. "John came to my rescue last night."

Completely ignoring the clock, she looked from Simon to John and back. But when her eyes did fall upon the clock, accidentally as it were, it seemed to have moved even closer to her plate.

"Indeed, Miss Evans, Mr. Britely was just telling me about the middle-of-the-night event. One never knows when Lady Joan will appear; especially when she's worried about something unusual. My advice, if you don't wish to encounter Lady Joan, is to stay in your room at night, for she has been known to roam the halls." He looked to John for affirmation, but John's gaze was on the clock.

Perhaps Simon was hesitant to offend a house guest, even an unwanted one, but John was not. He was bold to speak— "Have you any idea who could have left that clock on the floor in our hallway, Miss Evans? You were up so perhaps you saw something."

"What? A clock?" she asked with a fully innocent bearing. "Found where? In the hall? That *is* strange." She pretended not to notice the clock. Then the thought-of-all-thoughts visited her: "Lady Joan, your ghost, must have left it there. I guess I might have surprised her, and here I have been thinking she had surprised me." And Brenda began to eat as though the event, as she explained it, had been perfectly normal; had answered John's question.

But both his lordship and John knew Lady Joan had no interest in the clock, and couldn't have moved it.

XIII

Schrödinger Ails

Schrödinger was not well. He wouldn't move from his nap before the fire in the study. Moreover, Lord Haversham noticed that even after the fire was allowed to die, Schrödinger didn't move. At lunch, Schrödinger didn't arrive to sit on his tower to receive morsels that Lord Haversham might slip his way.

His lordship looked over at the empty tower. "Something isn't right with Schrödinger," he said. "He never fails to perch there when I'm here. John, please find a vet for Schrödinger."

"Simon, how you do go on about that cat," Lady Mardling said. "You'd think he was a member of your bloodline, an heir to the manor. He's just one ignoble feline amongst trillions. And a stray at that. Just wandered up, not even of noble blood, and with an absurd name."

Lady Mardling and Lady Southway had arrived for lunch.

Although despondent, his lordship knew life would have to go on, and sometimes hearing the silliness of these women convinced him that there was still something of interest to help fill a day without Emma. "Agnes," Lord Haversham said, "he may be one of trillions, but for some reason the universe has put me in charge of just this one, and I intend to do my best by him. Besides, the Egyptians found all cats to be quite noble. When Schrödinger originally graced us with his presence, Peter named him and whatever Peter thinks appropriate works for me and in fact at the time, Schrödinger secretly whispered to me that he liked his name." He had to laugh at his own folly; he loved to give these women a good razing, although the two women kept their appalled faces.

"I think that cat and Simon are tied at the umbilical cord," Brenda said. "I can understand that . . . Schrödinger is such a love. Though I've never petted him, I plan to. Simon, let me help you take him to the vet."

His lordship's laugh died quickly—for that burden of grief that was Emma's leaving—would always return to oppress him, and he couldn't bear thinking about another day with Miss Evans. It was difficult for him to converse with anyone now and, ignoring Miss Evans' request, he rose to leave. "Please excuse me, ladies. I have something urgent to attend to that will keep me busy until dinner."

At loose ends, he didn't know exactly how to fill that time, but he would find a way; lock himself in his library studying Proust for hours if he had to. The Ladies Mardling and Southway would just have to go to their homes, and Brenda would have to entertain herself in the best way she could find. He wasn't going to do it for her and he'd have to watch to avoid her, for he knew she would seek him out. First, he would see that Schrödinger was taken to the vet, then he would get the courage to tell Miss Evans her presence was not wanted at the manor. How to do that? Move her to the inn? He had commanded a regiment with no hesitation, yet speaking to that intimidating woman required a side of himself that wasn't practiced. Perhaps John could find a way. As well, he would redouble his efforts to get DCI Adams to run a television spot. The detectives weren't certain that Emma hadn't wanted to leave and had not wanted to be contacted. They didn't know her, he thought.

But before his lordship could exit the dining room, Brooks held the phone out to him.

"Sir, Detective Chief Inspector Adams on the phone for you."

"I'll take it in the study, please, Brooks."

"I'd like to know what it's about too, if you don't mind, Simon," Brenda said, "if it's about Emma." She jumped up to follow him.

He ignored her, but when he saw that Miss Evans had followed him into the study, he had to say, "I wish to speak in private." Let her think what she would; the woman was invasive.

After he shut her out, she leaned against the door to listen. Then she saw Brooks down the hall watching her, she laughed an evasive giggle and quickly turned toward the dining room as though—how could she be so silly? She just remembered she hadn't finished her lunch.

"Your Lordship, have you heard any more?" DCI Adams asked.

"No. Each day I feel sure I will hear from her with an explanation. I don't mind saying to you that she and I were growing quite close. I care for her deeply. Each day seems to bring a fresh remembrance of her, with assurance that she would not act this way. And each day something strange occurs. Mr. Tortle, of the law firm for which Ms. Chapman contracts, has called several times; he hasn't heard from her either. He firmly stands by Emma's character, and assures me that she would never drop an obligation."

"Another curiosity," he added. "She cherished a little gold clock that I gave her for Christmas. She would not have left without it, and yet she did. My housekeeper said the clock was found on an upper hallway floor." Lord Haversham waited for the pause while the detective thought about that; thought about that something abnormal.

"Miss Evans is the last person that you know of to have contact with Ms. Chapman?"

"Right."

"And as we know, Miss Evans' story is that Ms. Chapman said many things to her; an odd assortment of complaints, one of which was that she was unhappy with the contract coming up in London, that she thought of going home, or to an island. And that Ms. Chapman left during their hike to buy a journal in the village."

"Right. An odd assortment of issues completely alien to the Ms. Chapman I know."

"What do you know about Miss Evans?"

Lord Haversham was more than ever convinced now that having Miss Evans in the manor was not a good idea. He took a long breath to form his answer. What did he know about Miss Evans? "Very little," he said, "Nothing. Nothing to any certainty. She was kind enough to finish Ms. Chapman's contract in New York so she could take a trip here. It was about the third week in February. You might say that she owed Ms. Chapman a favor for covering for her when she took sick leave. Apparently Ms. Chapman knew her for only the few weeks of that contract, not before."

"How did Miss Evans come to be a guest at the manor?"

"When she called Ms. Chapman to tell her the work was finished, I was so pleased that Emma was here with me after we had been separated by misunderstandings, that I instantly issued the invitation for Miss Evans to come over to be my guest as well. So grateful to her for Ms. Chapman's opportunity to come here."

"And she accepted."

"Instantly."

"Why did Miss Evans take sick leave?"

"I've no idea."

"I think we should find out."

"Right. Right."

Now Schrödinger was clearly ill and he had given Lord Haversham such good care. Always seeking the room his lordship was in, always snoozing as close to him as possible, always accommodating his lordship by accepting proffered treats at meals—that now, his lordship applied himself to Schrödinger's health. John had located a veterinarian in Chipping Campden where he had an appointment for Schrödinger this very day. Regardless of the tragedy of Emma's disappearance, Schrödinger must have care, so Lord Haversham asked John please to take Schrödinger to Dr. Amundsen's clinic in Chipping Campden.

On the way to the clinic, with Schrödinger too ill to object to being carried off so, John drove up to speed, worrying all the way. "Hang on Schrödinger," he said, beseeching the cat not to give way. "We need you at the manor."

After examining Schrödinger, Dr. Amonsen said the cat had a common cat virus, and that he was sure Schrödinger would respond to antibiotics. The initial dose would be given now, and another in the morning. Schrödinger would have to stay over in his clinic for two days, one for the shots and one for follow-up to verify that indeed he was responding to treatment. "I'll call you tomorrow to let you know how the little fellow is getting on, and I believe it's quite likely that you can pick him up the next day."

John Britely drove back to Cav Neumont with a lighter heart. He, like his lordship, had come to think of Schrödinger as much a permanent and soothing fixture of the manor as was Lady Joan.

XIV

Josh

After Josh Chapman had called his mother the third time with no answer, he emailed Peter at college for Lord Haversham's phone number. Josh was acquainted with his lordship from the previous fall when he and his mother were guests at the manor. After Josh's technical skills had helped locate where a ring of criminals held Peter captive, thus providing the means for his rescue, the two lads had become great friends, spending their vacation time up in Peter's room (better known as the lab) developing software applications. But now, Josh's email to Peter crossed with his lordship's email to Peter to ask for Josh's phone number. Everyone wanted to ask everyone else whether he or she had heard from Emma. Up until now Josh hadn't been worried, for sometimes international mobile phone connections couldn't complete, but he had had no email from his mother either. Usually, she responded right away to his email. She had been at Cav Neumont Manor nearly two weeks now as a guest of Lord Haversham, so he would try to reach him. And when he did catch up to Simon, he learned the awful and mysterious truth: his mother hadn't been seen in three days.

Simon had taken Josh's call in the study. "It's true, Josh. In fact, I tried to reach you to hear whether you had a word from her. It seems she left in the midst of a hike. According to Miss Evans, the colleague who was hiking with her, she just turned around, said she wanted to buy a journal, and left, cutting across a field to a road off in the distance. Miss Evans also said that your mother wasn't looking forward to the London position, and might have returned to the States." Lord Haversham realized as he was saying this that he didn't believe it. But, sadly, most of Emma's things were gone as though she had planned to leave.

Josh had no way to know that each time Brenda told the story about his mother's leaving, her story grew longer; she thought of more details. "Doesn't sound right, that's not like Mom."

"Do you know Miss Evans?"

"No. I've heard of her through Aunt Ola, but only just."

"Has your Aunt Ola heard from your mother?"

"She hasn't. I just spoke with her." The universe seemed to halt in its journey while the airwaves listened to these transatlantic messages, as if indeed the whole universe wanted to know whether anyone had heard from Emma. "I've called the Free Title Company here in Manhattan," Josh said, "the one for which mother recently worked, and they've heard nothing. However, they hadn't expected to hear from her since she was not currently on a contract with them."

"I've called them as well," Lord Haversham said.

"Also, I asked to speak to mother's colleagues," Josh said, "and they said that one of them, Brenda Evans, had taken leave and was in England. So, I couldn't ask her whether she had heard from Mom. She must be the house guest you speak of."

"Right. She's here. I invited her here. She's the woman who saw your mother last—that we know of. It's her conviction that your mother hated the idea of her upcoming London contract."

"My mother never hated her contracts, and in particular, thrived on them. She especially enjoyed working for Tortle and Gainer. So as I needed to speak to someone who had recent contact with Mom, Free Title put me in touch with Luke Williams, and I have a meeting with him tomorrow. I hope to pick up any notion, any hint, that could lead to Mom."

"Miss Evans says your mother and Mr. Williams were close. I find that improbable."

"I agree. I've never heard her mention him. I'll find out something about that from the man himself, tomorrow. Meanwhile, what can we do next?"

"The detectives here are about to run a TV spot asking for any information," Lord Haversham said. "They've been reluctant to do this up to now, believing Miss Evans' story may have some credibility. They have to consider the possibility that your mother *wanted* to leave. But since she has not turned up anywhere, or contacted any of us, and after they've listened to Mr. Tortle and me, they're finally convinced that she wouldn't have left without a word."

"Absolutely not! I want to come over, but I don't know what good that would do. I could walk the trails, but for what purpose?"

"Right. You're welcome though, Josh. Anytime. You know that. Your presence would lend me moral support at this dark time. I can't imagine that your mother would have wanted to leave like this. Josh, let's keep in touch, and do come over if you can."

And before his lordship disconnected, Brenda came into the room. She almost leapt forward, almost took the phone from his hand before she caught herself and stopped. "I want to talk to him."

Lord Haversham abhorred yielding to her on any point; still, he wanted to hear what she would say to Josh. He handed her the phone.

"You'll probably hear from your mother soon," Brenda said to Josh, using her perky tone. "I'll bet she's just having fun somewhere, too busy to contact you, off in some place like Bora Bora before she has to return to the States and to work." Head back, she gave Simon a knowing, teasing look. "Your mother told me she wanted to go somewhere—to a desert island for a change. You know it rains here most of the time, and she said she didn't want to work in London." Brenda had thought this and told it so many times that saying it was making it true.

Josh could *hear* her cavalier smile.

In the long silence over the phone, Brenda could hear Josh's thoughts. "It's not worth your while to come over here," she said, "for your mother left no message and no definite indication where she was going. I'm sure she'll call you soon. You're just a mamma's boy, aren't you? Expecting to be forever in touch with her. You're a big boy, Josh. We've all heard about your work for the FBI."

Lord Haversham had heard enough. He took the phone from her, disconnected the call, and left the room. Left her standing, mouth open ready to make another foul remark.

What an outrageous thing for her to say, Josh thought. Even so, he was not happy with *anything* she said. Not just because he hadn't heard from his mother, but as well there was something slimy about Miss Evans. He hadn't met her, and yet he could feel that she radiated an underlying pleasure of some sort that had to do with his mother's leaving. He could hear an undercurrent of happiness in Brenda's soul that Emma had left without telling anyone where, or why, or goodbye. Why was she happy? He had an unpleasant, uncomfortable feeling listening to her. And who was she, anyway? He didn't think his mother had known her well, or for long. He would call Aunt Ola again. Emma kept close contact with her, but when he reached Ola, she told him she had still not heard from Emma. It had been about a week, she said since she had talked to Emma. She knew Emma was busy, but really, she would have called by now just to check in.

"This is just plain weird," Ola said, "I couldn't be more worried, for we know that your mother and Lord Haversham were deeply fond of each other; seemed to be growing more so all the time. I had been thinking we might lose your dear mother to England."

"Well, despite that woman's telling me there was no point in my going over there, if I don't hear from Mom soon, I'll have to. I have to talk to Lord Haversham directly; hear whatever he can think of. Perhaps I'll call him again tomorrow." Josh and his Great Aunt Ola disconnected their phones after agreeing that either one would call the other soon, and with any news.

Indeed, Emma's disappearance wasn't normal. Aside from his worry about her, and the stress that caused, Josh's college funds were running out and soon he would have to apply to Aunt Ola for financial help; that is if he could concentrate enough to stay in college; his mother would want that. And anyway, what else was he to do? The point was, that Josh knew his mother would never neglect providing for his college. As it was, he had only a small income from the FBI for his part-time technology work.

In the end, the suspense proved to be too much for Josh; he couldn't concentrate. Not content to stay in school while there had been no word from his mother in a week, Josh flew to England to seek her wherever he could.

Lord Haversham would receive no guest now, except Miss Evans—staying on under DCI Adams' directive—but his lordship welcomed Josh as family. His grief extended to Josh, for whom he felt incalculable pain. He remembered the friendly and intelligent interaction that he had witnessed last fall between Josh and his mother when they had been his guests. But it was not in his power to ease Josh's pain; could only tell him that Emma had seemed quite happy: happy with the new contract in London, happy to be again at the manor. He knew she was happy to be with him; every look, every touch, and every utterance from her was a caress for him. Could he have been so wrong? She had said nothing about leaving or being discontent.

On his first day at the manor Josh wanted to hear from Brenda exactly what she knew, and he drilled her down, making her repeat her tales until perspiration sprouted across her forehead. But she wasn't about to buckle under and she told pretty much the confusing mixture of stories that all along she had said to Lord Haversham and the detectives; except, if anything, she grew more determined in her opinion that Emma had wanted to leave and had said so. Though some of her answers to Josh's questions seemed uncertain at times. Surely she had practiced her story enough by now, but perhaps she was intimidated by Josh's forbidding opacity. Did he believe her? She couldn't tell. He wanted to know exactly what his mother had carried with her on the hike. Had she taken her laptop? If not, where was it? Had she taken her mobile phone, her wallet, her passport? If not, where were they? All questions Brenda had already answered numerous times for the detectives. She didn't know, she said, where those items were. This pest would have to turn up now, she bemoaned to herself, when people seemed to be getting used to Emma's absence, and Simon was a bit more polite at times.

So, on the second day, Josh started along Neumont Path, the public trail that Brenda said she and his mother had taken for their hike. As he went, he beat along from side to side with his walking stick, looking for anything, any clue, even any step off the trail that would indicate that someone had taken a detour. Neumont Path extended easterly from the manor nearly seven miles, curving around slightly until it hit the high road through the village of Cav Neumont. His hike took most of the day and he saw and heard nothing that could have been a clue to Emma's disappearance. When Josh reached the village, he circled back west toward the manor, stopping at shops as he went, showing the proprietors a photograph of his mother. But at the stationer's, and at the inns, and at the pub, no one had seen her recently. Certainly she had not come in for a journal. At the inns he was told to come back in the evening when a different shift was on, and inquire again.

A salesclerk in a dress shop said the photo was familiar, but the woman of whom she was reminded, lived on a farm in another county, and was a farmer working the farmers' market; couldn't have been the same woman. And as well, the woman in the photo had a different hairstyle, looked younger; when she thought about it—really could hardly be the same person.

Josh arrived back at the manor in time for dinner, having missed tea. He had no stomach for eating, but he went in to dinner with Simon, John, and Brenda. Any remark of theirs might be another clue. "Today I could find nothing that might relate to Mom," he said. "To begin with I thought my hike would perhaps be a waste of time, but I had to do something, I couldn't just sit here, or sit in school unable to concentrate."

"I completely understand," Lord Haversham said. "Bud, Major, and I scoured Neumont thoroughly ourselves. As well, we roamed the direct shot through the woods, that area between Neumont Path and the town road. Miss Evans said that Emma left the path, so exactly how she reached the village road . . . if she did . . . is unknown."

"That's true, Simon," Brenda said. "After we had walked for a while, Emma discovered that we were on the wrong trail for bluebells. Perhaps that's when she decided that she might as well make for the journal."

"Bluebells? You were looking for *bluebells*, Miss Evans?" his lordship asked. "So all along it had been Ms. Chapman's intent to see the bluebells?"

Even though she was more expert as the days went by in covering for herself, this had been a slip on Brenda's part, for the huge field of bluebells was off Bingers Trail, not Neumont. She had no choice, now that the bluebell subject had been brought up, but to say, "Yes." She hoped she wouldn't have to elaborate.

"I thought surely Ms. Chapman knew bluebells were mainly off Bingers," his lordship said. "Not Neumont. Indeed, she seemed content to see our own fields . . . in particular right off our front entrance, a view from her room."

His demanding look pierced Brenda forcing her to firmly end, if she could, this topic. "She did lead me to Neumont Path with the intention of hiking along to a bluebell field." She cast her face into firm assurance.

During this exchange an idea grew on Josh: he would have to hike along Bingers. Brenda hadn't been here long—perhaps she was disoriented, wrong about exactly which trail she and his mother had taken. And there was something wrong about Brenda, something unzipped about her concern for his mother: she was too unconcerned, always on the verge of flirting with Simon; not something a person would easily slip into in this situation. Clearly she must sense Simon's loss, and yet, it was as though she were waiting for his lordship to ease up and pay her the attention she deserved. And she was thoughtlessly casual toward his own worry about his mother.

"I'll hike Bingers tomorrow, sir."

"I'll join you," his lordship said. "I hadn't thought of looking there, since Miss Evans said they had been on Neumont, but now that the mention of bluebells comes up . . . we should look in another direction, and it will be better than continuing to wait here. We'll take Major; he needs a good long romp. He's also at a loss for your mother. She and I were working on his training."

Brenda felt only a mild unease with this information; surely there would be no tracks leading to Emma's body, or to her buried passport, wallet, and phone. She felt safe in the knowledge that they could walk Bingers forever without finding a trace of Emma. Even with that stupid dog.

In the morning Lord Haversham and Josh set out for Bingers. On their way it was hard not to find a funny bone while watching Major dart away up the trail, then back, four legs spinning faster than a top. Hurry up slow pokes, his eyes said each time he circled back to the men, then off to the left, back, off to the right, then back: *hurry up*. And in between sniffing as many molded leaves and twigs along the way as he could fit in and still keep on the move. His lordship had no fear as they hiked, that Major would run too far or get lost: not ten seconds would pass without Major checking a glance back to secure his tie to his lordship.

Bingers was not easy going and not often hiked because the landowner spent no effort grooming the narrow trail. So the man and young man walked slowly, beating their walking sticks about the brush along the trailside, looking for clues that related to Emma. They had brought snacks: carrot sticks, apples, cheese, coffee, water, dog biscuits, and after two hours or so of strenuous moving, they stopped to eat.

"Up ahead I can show you the drop-off where your mother fell last fall and was stranded for three days."

"And we have you to thank for finding her," Josh replied. "Now, if you can just find her again."

"Right." His lordship drew a deep sigh: indeed, if he only could. He knew, though he hadn't exactly said so to Emma, that he wanted to spend all his days with her. Why hadn't he told her unequivocally? The deepest emotions took their time developing; he felt so, and he knew her to feel the same—why they were quite at ease together—neither conferring obligation or pressure on the other. And after his marriage to Claire, when he had let her rush him into marriage, so taken up with her exquisite face and bubbly laughter, as he had been, only to realize in less than a year the far reach of his mistake: a short engagement might have long, unwanted, consequences. What could he think now? Had Emma wanted to leave him? No. Not without a word. That would be breaking every convention he knew she believed in.

Major waited patiently at their feet while they sat on a log and ate; well, perhaps not so patiently in between dog biscuits and bites of lunch dropped on purpose, and the cup of water set down for him, and squeals to be up and off on the trail again, nearly wagging off his tail. He sensed there was something dire about this journey, but how dire could you be when there was so much here to discover?

Then, from up ahead, a man pushed through the brush toward them. "Hello. Surprising to see someone on Bingers. I'm Andy Sullivan," and he would have reached out a hand, but for seeing that the two men were eating.

"I'm Simon and this is Josh. I'm happy to see another soul here; not used to seeing another hiker on Bingers. As you said."

"I'm here for archaeological research for my thesis," Andy said. "Combining that with hiking. I was at Cav Neumont in the fall with a hiking group, got a feel for the area, and decided to come back for some solo hikes; I love this part of England, but this is a rough trail. Last fall, one of our hikers fell off a cliff near here and came close to not being rescued. And although the woman lives in New York, someone at the inn said they had heard she was back. I thought she might enjoy hiking with me; however, I haven't been able to find out where she is."

Josh wondered how much Simon wanted to say. He would let Simon lead, and he looked to him and waited. Simon paused for so long he seemed to consult a woods oracle for what to say, how much to say. The very pores of the trees expanded to catch what came next. Even Major caught the import of the pause and grew quiet. Lord Haversham found a place to speak.

"We're looking for her. Emma." His face drew into such sadness.

Andy heard the moan pulled up from somewhere deep in his lordship's being. "That's right . . . Emma Chapman."

"She left us. She has been staying with us at the manor but we haven't heard from her in over a week now. Not like her at all. I'm her close friend. Josh is her son."

The woods were still while Andy studied the men and thought about what Simon said. "Although I only know her from a hiking tour, I wouldn't think that would be like her at all," he said. Lord

Haversham and Josh packed away their lunch bits while Andy waited, trying to absorb this strange information.

"Would you care to join us?" Simon asked. "We can always use another pair of eyes. We're walking and looking . . . looking for clues. Then afterward come back with us to the manor for dinner."

"Are you Lord Haversham then?" Andy asked.

"The same."

"I would be honored." Andy thought to tell his lordship that on a tour through the manor last fall, he had met the resident ghost, and how it had scared him quite senseless on his way to the loo. But the seriousness of this situation forbade mentioning it. "Was Emma last seen on Bingers?" he asked.

"No. Her colleague, Miss Evans, said that she and Emma were hiking along Neumont Path on the other side of the village. However, later on Miss Evans also said that they sought the bluebells field, which is about a half-mile on up ahead," he gestured. "So, perhaps Miss Evans was mistaken about which trail they took. And we find it difficult to do nothing but wait. No one has heard from Emma in nearly a week now, neither her employer not her aunt in New York, with whom she was careful to keep in touch. Her aunt is worried to the point of being ill. As I almost am myself."

Major saw that something would happen now; the three men took up their hiking sticks and set to the trail. Now he had three men to admire his expert circling back, for the new man had petted him fondly.

Soon the waft of blue drifted skyward signaling its nearness. You could not have missed it: even tucked among oaks and ashes, the ground was solid blue nearly as far as you could see in all directions. They stopped. They stared. For translucent as crystal, Lady Joan hovered there, just over the bluebells. The very air was blue and hazy, and on occasion Lady Joan was herself blue and hazy. "What the . . .," Lord Haversham started. What was real and what was not? It was hard to say. Uncertain what to think or what to do next, the three men waited for some signal. Had Emma reached this far? Miss Evans said that Emma had headed for a road. There was no road near here.

"I want to walk into the field a bit," Simon said, taking his cue from Lady Joan. And with careful steps, he started through the blue bells. Major romped ahead, way into the bluebells. He could almost not be seen, so thick was the blue cover. His lordship pressed on, Josh and Andy following. Now they couldn't see Major at all; he was deep into the field. Had Emma been here? There was no sign. And if she had turned and hiked out in another direction, which way would that have been? Only one way led back to the manor, the way they had come, and another led back to their village. Had she taken any other direction? Only the angels would know where she had gone—and perhaps Lady Joan.

Lord Haversham gestured with his hiking stick. "If she walked out that direction, she would reach Wethermere, but miles away, perhaps twenty or more. Otherwise there's nothing around except Chipping Campden, and that's even farther."

Now there was no sign of Major. Lord Haversham raised a quieting finger to his lips and asked, "Where is Major?"

Josh and Andy listened quietly. No sound except a faint rustling among the overhead branches as a breeze came around to listen.

"Major," Lord Haversham called. Then they saw off in the distance, the dog's tail bobbing about. Digging. It looked like he was digging. "Major," his lordship called again. Major continued excitedly digging at something, working his paws, tail, and rump in the air.

"I'll walk over to see what's keeping him," his lordship said. "Must be very interesting for him not to come when called." He stretched out over the bells twenty paces or so to where his fine dog was eagerly digging, and when he reached Major the unintelligible yell that pushed and heaved up from Simon's core quivered the trees and shook the earth; sent chills through Josh and Andy, who froze on the spot. Clasped within Major's teeth was a wallet. Simon took it from the dog and with trembling fingers, opened it. Emma's identification stared up at him. He shook. His hands and legs trembled until he dropped the wallet and bowed his face into his hands. By now Josh and Andy, with fearful, tentative steps, had caught up to him and saw the wallet drop. The three men looked at the hole Major had dug, and there lay Emma's mobile phone and passport. Lord Haversham put his hand on Major to still the dog, stop his digging, let him know he had done well. "Good boy," he choked out, and he picked up the three items, holding them carefully as though they were jewels, or perhaps a part of Emma. Josh and Andy stared silently. Josh's eyes filled with tears as he looked up at Simon to see that his eyes were tearing as well. Without speaking, they began to look around. The bluebells covered several acres and soon it would be dark.

"We must turn back. Soon it will be too dark to see anything," Lord Haversham said. It was almost a whisper. "I'll let Detective Chief Inspector Adams know what we've found . . . I'll call him as soon as we reach the manor, and tomorrow I'll show him Emma's things." His voice broke. "And, I'll be sure to show him to this place so he can send out a search team. With my help."

"Gentlemen, please let us not mention this back at the manor. Let's keep this to ourselves until I speak to DCI Adams, hear his opinion, and until we know more."

With heavy hearts, they turned back toward Cav Neumont, each stumbling step like the dark lament of a drumbeat somewhere.

"Any calls, Brooks?" His lordship leaned on Brooks' arm to move up the steps. Always hopeful, he expected that either Emma would be waiting for them, a plausible explanation happily flowing over him, or a phone call from her had come in saying she had been locked in an elevator, something, anything to know that she was alright. But when Brooks replied, "No sir," Lord Haversham said, "Ah . . ." then, "Brooks, we have a guest," and he gestured to Andy. "Please have Mrs. Penrose make up a room for Mr. Sullivan, if he will stay. He's a friend of Ms. Chapman's."

"Hello all," Brenda said. "It's such a lovely evening. How did your hike on Bingers go?" When no one replied, she said, "Look at all the long faces. It must have been a struggle. . . exactly why Emma and I didn't hike Bingers."

She had no idea that the men had indeed found Emma's buried personal items. She would not have expected the possibility, as she had buried them far from where any human would roam. She hadn't considered the non-human, Major. Her chipper tone rose up to assault Simon. He might look sour, even pained, but she wouldn't let that interfere; he shouldn't think that she felt guilty. She felt solid in her place here. He was alone now that she had gotten rid of Emma, and he was lonely; she would win him over. She was just what he needed and not too long from now he would come to feel his need for her. She knew how to work his emotions, and had the wiles to do so.

No one replied. Lord Haversham acted as though she hadn't spoken. He poured his sherry and passed the bottle to Josh. Then taking his glass with him, he excused himself to go to his room. Let this woman go home. If she didn't go on her own, if DCI Adams didn't release her, he would have to push her out; get a room at the inn for her, if it came to that. He could not bear to look at her. He had never before had to be so rude. Miss Evans would have to remain in the dark about what was transpiring.

However, Brenda was not to remain in the dark, for in the morning when the search team gathered at Cav Neumont Manor, Brenda was waiting nearby, and though the briefing had been behind closed doors, on their departure she overheard two of them discussing those items of Emma's that Lord Haversham had found on Bingers the day before, and that they were to search the bluebell field. She didn't panic though; felt very much in control. Her firm story was that she had never been on Bingers; let anyone prove differently. How could she know how Emma's things got in the field of bluebells? Emma could have hidden her things there herself; maybe she wanted a new identity. When she thought about it, all kinds of options presented themselves. Perhaps this new guest, Andy, off'd Emma. The detectives would have to consider that; doesn't the perp often return to the crime scene? And hadn't they met Andy on Bingers?

When DCI Adams and Lord Haversham were ready to set out for Bingers, it was decided that only his lordship should accompany DCI Adams and his men. Too many on that narrow, rough trail would slow their progress, and besides, his lordship knew the trail better than anyone. Although it wasn't on his land, he had grown up in that area and had hiked all the land around many, many times. So Josh and Andy stayed behind, trying to avoid Brenda.

But, when they sat for lunch, she insisted on regaling them with her own reasons for Emma's things having been found in that field, none of which were convincing. She herself had never walked on Bingers, she said. She had only hiked on Neumont. Maybe, she suggested, Emma left Neumont, hiked over to Bingers, and intending to take up a new identity, had buried her ID. Certainly far-fetched, but after all, she didn't have a crystal ball. "I only know for certain what Emma told me," she said.

Lord Haversham and DCI Adams' search team returned from the exploration with feelings needing to be sorted out. No further trace of Emma had been found. His lordship flailed between thinking that was a good thing, and wondering what it could mean.

XV

Brenda Evans' History

Brenda Evans had a history that had been kept private, a bipolar history. If she didn't stay on medication her actions became unpredictable; perhaps at times even dangerous, especially when things weren't going her way. By working as a freelance legal aide, she had avoided close employer scrutiny, so no one knew. Luke Williams knew though, for they had begun to live together. What Brenda lacked in stability, she gained in beauty. Her slender and graceful frame, finished with a perfect oval face and silken blonde tresses, had learned to belie her instability, gloss it over, as it were.

While working together at the Free Title Company, they had grown close. He loved her face. At first, they had lunches together, then dinners, and then they were going home together. He thought Brenda was his perfect match—bubbly, not taking anything too seriously. Then one evening Brenda burned their dinner and flew into a rage. Perhaps had had too much wine, Luke wondered. He tried to console her.

"It's not your fault," he had said. "I distracted you when we were fooling around. I take all blame." And he laughed at her—then was surprised that he was unable to help her see the silliness of being so upset.

"I hate it!" she had screamed at him. "I hate you!" She reached for a knife and came at him with it. As she thrashed about, he grabbed her arms and held her until she tired. He twisted her wrist until she dropped the knife. Then he flung her around, gripping her tightly from behind while he dialed 911. After that, she spent seventy-two hours in lock-up, and when she was released, Luke was told to make sure she stayed on her medication.

Those seventy-two hours were the days that Emma, on a contract at the same company, had covered for Brenda, finished up Brenda's title searches and closings. But Luke had not said why Brenda was on sick leave. Then later, back at work and stable for the time being, Brenda covered for Emma so she could take a trip to Chipping Campden at a time when, thanks to Lady Claire's mischievous chicanery, Emma had felt estranged from Simon. It had not been Emma's intention at all to stay in Cav Neumont, but Lord Haversham had found her at the library in Chipping Campden. Josh had told him he could likely find her there. That trip had reunited them, and later provided Lord Haversham's enthusiastic invitation to Brenda to come join Emma and him; be his guest at the manor. He was grateful to have Emma back. "Miss Evans covered for you so you could come back into my life," he had said to Emma at the time. "I want to show Miss Evans my appreciation."

But neither Emma nor Lord Haversham knew Brenda's history, or that she had to stay on medication and restrict her wine intake. They didn't know that Luke had called Brenda several times to make certain she was taking her medication. She wasn't. She had stopped—convinced that she was in control of her sanity; knew perfectly well how to behave. Had found what she wanted at the manor.

XVI

Emma at the Veterinarian's

Something pulled at Emma, that sensation again, something on the brink of recognition. She and Mars sat in the veterinarian's waiting room with Harvey, holding his lead close. Mars had noticed that Harvey had been running with a slight limp, and so he had brought the dog in to have his leg examined. Harvey panted with anxiety, seemingly aware that this place was all about *him*, and that was not good. Emma joined him in listening to howling dogs and cat pleas coming from in back somewhere. In particular one cat plea rose above the rest. That was the one that pulled at Emma, or seemed to. Puzzling.

With Harvey on the examining table now, you could see his effort at bravery. Whatever was to happen, he stood sturdily against it, but would face it with courage as long as Mars and Emma were witnesses. His countenance bore the knowledge that his friends, ever loyal, had never been known to allow harm to creatures of any kind.

Emma continued to hear that plaintive meow. Then it was time for Harvey's exam, and while Dr. Amonsen, worked his fingers down Harvey's leg, Emma asked, "May I look at the cats? I love them so. They fascinate me."

"We have only one staying over right now. He's been in quarantine for flu, but he's well enough to go home tomorrow." Dr. Amonsen opened a door for Emma and said, "He's down the hall just inside that door there on the right."

Emma went down the hall to the door Doc Amonsen had pointed out. Why was she doing this, she wondered. She liked cats but not to the point of going out of her way to see one unknown to her. But again she heard the cry. When she opened the door and saw Schrödinger, she felt a blow. This cat—this cat was special. She petted him through the cage and Schrödinger stroked against her fingers as best he could. He purred. He seemed to say, you're here for me. *Schrödinger*. His name was taped above his cage. The name stuck in Emma's thoughts. "I know your name," she said. "Schrödinger." But she couldn't figure out why she knew it.

Back in the examining room, Doctor Amonsen was busy explaining to Mars about Harvey's injury. "Just a sprain. Better not to let him run for a week or so. Walk him on a lead."

He was applying tape around Harvey's ankle when Emma softly asked, "Who owns that cat?"

But now Dr. Amonsen wanted to show Mars something about changing the tape, should he need to. "Some dogs have great fun wallowing in mud if they get a chance. But I see you are too much of a gentleman for that activity," he said to Harvey, giving the dog a good, firm petting. Released, Harvey pulled so fast out the door that Emma's question went unanswered. It's probably a silly idea anyway, she thought—as she followed Harvey on the run—that she would remember that cat. Still, she did seem to know him. Harvey jumped into the car, licked Mars' ear, and gave Mars a look that said, *Thank you, Mars. Thank you for saving me from that place of torture. I'm your servant forever.*

Dr. Amonsen popped his head out the door and called, "Lord Haversham." But he saw their car driving off. Well, she didn't hear,

but he probably shouldn't be giving out that information anyway. He wondered why she was curious.   Emma was quiet on the ride back to the farm. That cat seemed to know her. But that idea merely added to the many others trying to press through to memory—enough to keep her in a quandary.

XVII

Lady Claire at Wickenbird Farm

Lord Haversham had just handed his fine horse, Bud, over to Hadley when a Mercedes SUV pulled around the circle. Lady Claire Haversham's chauffeur stepped out of the car and opened the door for her. She removed her slender, elegant and perfumed frame from the vehicle and, head turned up with an imperious side-glance at Simon said, "Hello, dear, I'm on my way to Wickenbird Farm—over near Wethermere—and thought I'd pop in. Perhaps for sherry, if you'll indulge me." She noticed his sad, long-drawn face, not like his nature at all.

His lordship looked hard at the Mercedes, words slow to form, but thoughts rapidly building up regarding the expense Claire was incurring. "You know, Claire, that your budget is fixed, unalterable."

"Dear, do not worry about the car, I have not bought it, just leased it for the day with this exquisite chauffeur." She turned to the driver who, dressed in dark livery and looking trim and quite refined, acknowledged her comment with a sticky smile. "Isn't he adorable?" she said, touching his chin with a delicate finger. "You see, Simon, in the back I have two very old wicker chairs that I'm taking for repairs. That's the requirement for the large car."

Claire's title, 'Lady' was only a courtesy, officially lost to her with her divorce from his lordship. Years back when she and Lord Haversham married, she had moved into the manor with her young son, Peter, then took off around the world leaving his lordship to raise the boy. Following their divorce, she continued to entertain herself at casinos and ski slopes, lavishly spending more than she could afford—even with his lordship's generous settlement. Years later, ladened with debts and disappointments, she wanted to return to him, to live again at the manor. In fact, she just arrived one day, unannounced, with a year's worth of belongings, and an intention to stay. She was Peter's mother, and the boy needed his mother. (The boy in question was already eighteen-years-old.) His lordship had given her his firm assurance that her living at the manor again was impossible. Still, she had tried to work her way back into his life, and had used underhanded tricks and devious wiles in the effort; tried to separate him from Emma, a guest at the manor, and whom Lady Claire saw as the enemy. She had witnessed clear signs that Lord Haversham's heart belonged to Emma. Therefore, to control Lady Claire's spending and keep her distant, Lord Haversham had set her up in a townhouse in London, and thereafter he and John managed her expenses within an extremely fixed budget. For Peter's sake, he wanted to assure that Claire did not fail.

Ironic, he thought, that now Claire wouldn't have to struggle to part him from Emma. So now, he could tolerate Claire for tea or sherry, and that was it.

"Wickenbird Farm? Is there not in the vast expanse of London a wicker worker?"

"Not for these chairs. The seats are made of a rare willow and cane, which I want replaced exactly, and by hand."

"I see. Classic. Yes, of course, Claire, we shall have a sherry together." He asked Hadley to take her driver in for refreshment, then, without offering Lady Claire his arm, stood by for her to precede him up the steps into the manor.

It annoyed him that Claire now sat in Emma's favorite chair by the fireplace. Her usual flirty self (why hadn't that bothered his sensitivities before they married) displayed as much leg as decency would allow. With nothing on his mind that he wanted to say to her, he waited for her to lead their conversation.

Her eyes swept over the room touching on the appointments here and there, old and new. "I don't see the little gold clock, Simon," she said, delicately sipping sherry. She had tried to take the clock for herself last fall. "Where is it? What's happened to it?"

He couldn't answer. What could he say? Definitely not that it had been found in mysterious circumstances on the floor in an upper hallway, and now was locked up with other precious items.

"Simon, you're quite sedate. Do you have to think about where the clock is?"

Claire didn't know that he had given it to Emma for her Christmas gift, and he didn't want to go into explanations with her. It wasn't her concern. Emma's disappearance wasn't her concern, and Claire, he knew, would make good use of that information. He thought of what he could say to satisfy her, *it began to lose time, and is in London for cleaning.* But it wasn't in his nature to invent in such a way; he would rather be straight with people, easier to explain and worked more satisfactorily in the outcome. So, he said instead, "Tell me about the farm to which you're headed."

Claire knew better than to press Lord Haversham on a point—knew that he would not yield, and so she thought it wiser to let the subject change. "A farmer at Wickenbird Farm has a hobby, side-line, if you will, of caning. He's quite well known for it, and runs a small ad from time to time. And I have these lovely old wicker chairs . . . I adore wicker . . . that are springing apart here and there."

"I see."

"I thought I would have a lovely day's outing taking the chairs out to the farm. Then on another day I'll have another outing to fetch them."

"Fair enough."

"That might be in winter, I understand, for the farmer is busy with the farm until then." She adjusted her skirt, sipped sherry, then drummed her fingers and gave him a steadying look, while waiting for his response. "You're not yourself today, Simon. Is something troubling you? Not Peter, I trust."

With her son, Peter, usually away at college, she and he had little contact with each other, although Lord Haversham always assured them that the doors were open for them to meet. Peter understood. He knew his mother had scarcely wanted to be at the manor until last fall when she had come back, begging—quite in debt.

Simon searched for reasons to give Claire for his lethargy and was about to ask her, by way of avoiding the question, what she had been doing lately, when he was saved the trouble by an interruption: Miss Evans came into the room. Unfortunate that she had to come in, he thought, an awkward mix of his unwanted guests. For in view of DCI Adams' requirement that Miss Evans stay in town, his lordship had been stalling in finding a way to evict her. Moreover, there was his overriding hope that Emma would come home (he wanted to think of the manor as her home). Then DCI Adams would release Miss Evans, and he could send her packing.

"Simon, I've been looking all over for you," Brenda said. "Brooks said you had come in. I never expected to find you in the drawing room so early. Sherry? I'll have one myself." She looked at Claire.

"Claire," Lord Haversham said, "this is Miss Brenda Evans. Miss Evans this is Lady Claire." He hoped the topic of what troubled him would end there. Didn't want to give explanations. Still, he knew that was a futile desire. Put those two inquisitive, invasive women in the same room—*Lord help me*.

"It's a pleasure to meet you, Lady Claire," Brenda said, helping herself to sherry. "Please call me Brenda. I'm trying to train Simon to call me Brenda; he doesn't need to be so formal with me." This was an acquaintance good to know, she thought, as she scanned her ladyship's expensive coif, very stylish silk tunic with gold tassels, and gold bracelets lining her arms. *And she had a title!*

Lady Claire barely nodded, too taken up in noticing that Simon didn't pour Miss Evans' sherry. Not up to his usual proper manners, though he did half stand when Miss Evans entered. Claire had heard from Lady Mardling that Ms. Chapman was back at the manor despite Claire's scaring her off, and that another American would arrive shortly to compete for Simon's attentions. Well, this one was certainly pretty enough, although there was that certain commonness about her, Claire thought. Slurps her sherry. Refers to him as Simon, though he seems to wish that she would not. Still, she might explore what Miss Evans has to offer. Lately, Lady Mardling had had no news for Claire about goings-on at the manor, except that his lordship was keeping to himself, making all kinds of excuses, and the vulgar sort of American woman had arrived. This Miss Evans must be the woman about whom Lady Mardling referred, Lady Claire thought. This could get interesting.

"It's quite a ride to Wethermere," Lord Haversham said. He used his warning voice, hoping to send Claire on her way. "I believe it's nearly to Chipping Campden. Shouldn't you be off?"

"What happens in Wethermere?" Brenda spoke up, heedless of being invasive.

Lady Claire was about to ignore her question, but then she thought that perhaps she could say a bit more to this intrusive American without harm to herself, as well as to find a use for her and so she said, "Chairs, Miss Evans. Chairs. I'm dropping off wicker chairs there to be renewed. The farmer is a caner. The chairs are too old and lovely to leave in the hands of just anyone." She thought the American looked capable of great rudeness, but she wasn't expecting a question such as that which followed.

"Might I come along?" Brenda asked. "I would love to see the countryside." More to the point, though, was her desire for the social connection.

It took Lady Claire's indignation just three seconds to slide from the level to which Brenda's question had raised it—where she was ready to say, *Impossible. I won't be returning back this way*—to a better thought: Miss Evans might be a useful source of gossip, someone to manipulate. So she said, "I would be delighted to have you along, my dear. Simon, would you call Brooks to send round my car?" Then she wondered aloud, "Where *is* Ms. Chapman? I've heard from Agnes that Ms. Chapman was back."

Lord Haversham would have found a way to avoid Claire's question, but Miss Evans was ready with a quick reply.

"Oh, Emma has left us!" Brenda said, her self-importance lifting to new heights. "Indeed, high and dry. Not a word. We've had no word from her."

Although one of the most non-violent men in the kingdom, still Lord Haversham could have clocked her. He had to get out of the room. And rising to signal the conversation was over, he said, "Claire, Brooks will see you out."

"Simon! Ms. Chapman has left! And suddenly! Without a word! Why, Simon . . . I find that amusing. Did the two of you have words?"

He merely said, "Appearances are not what they seem, Claire." He would not give her the dignity of an explanation. "I believe your driver is waiting, and this is not a convenient time for me to converse. Would you ladies please excuse me, I have work to do." But his dodge fell on Claire's suspicious ears.

All attempts to keep Emma's absence as private news would have failed to remain private anyway, for very shortly the manor's Ellie had told Lady Agnes Mardling's maid, Smith, that she hadn't seen Ms. Chapman in four or five days—and like an echo devilishly eager to repeat it—Lady Mardling would soon enough spread that news through her web. Ah, Lady Mardling had thought, that explains why she hadn't seen Ms. Chapman on her last visit to the manor, and possibly why Simon was isolating himself lately. When she heard that intriguing morsel from Smith, her upper eyelids were stuck in the extreme open position for the remainder of the day. And she couldn't get to Simon for explanation, for he had made himself unavailable. She didn't know the worst of it: that Emma had left without so much as a *goodbye-and-see-you-soon*.

In any case, his lordship had feared that Lady Mardling would soon hear this from Claire. The two women wove a web of gossip that stretched from Cav Neumont to London, and he would eventually have to endure acerbic remarks from all the women. And, as soon as he could he would remove Miss Evans from the manor—one way or another. If Emma didn't return, he might just go back to Lake Como to try to heal his heart. This time though, except for Peter, his adopted son, and John, and Brooks, and his most trusted staff, no one would know where he was.

Lady Claire's self-satisfied grin lasted all the way from Cav Neumont Manor to Wickenbird Farm. It was a cinch to bond instantly with the so-eager Miss Evans. Lady Claire waited a decent period of time, speaking only about the day, the weather, the lovely peace of the countryside, before asking about Ms. Chapman's departure as though it were only of incidental interest.

"Oh no one knows what happened to her," Brenda said. "No one has heard. She and I were hiking Neumont, when she suddenly left the trail, left me alone, said she had to go to the village to buy a journal." Brenda had told her story so many times now, she sounded confident with information, no longer hesitantly finding the words to sound convincing. And now she throve with the surprised look on Lady Claire's face; this new acquaintance held promise for gratification. There hadn't been enough people to give her the attention she deserved, and Lady Claire seemed ready to make a donation.

"And Lord Haversham hasn't heard from her?"

"Not that anyone knows . . . I'm sure of it. When I came in from hiking that afternoon, just in time for tea, he asked where she was. All of us expected her to come in any minute, but she didn't. Not ever. Simon won't rest and detectives have been out to interview us."

"Detectives!" Lady Claire erupted. "Indeed! I tried to warn him about Ms. Chapman's devious character, but he wouldn't listen. You know how men are: stubborn, quite satisfied with their own intuition against all evidence to the contrary."

"Oh, I know about Emma's character. I have first-hand experience with her. I worked with her in New York, and that firm was happy to see the last of her."

Lady Claire had met in Brenda her match for deviousness. She suspected that this slander was pure invention, but it served her own needs to receive it as truth.

"Simon invited me here . . . that is . . . through Emma. I had had to complete her work in New York." Her eyes rolled up and around. "And he wanted to thank me in person. Turns out that's not all he wanted."

Lady Claire's eyes formed a large question mark as she waited for more.

Brenda had stumbled on new slander to bandy about. "I probably shouldn't say this, but he's been giving me unwanted attention. I try to be careful not to be in the room alone with him.

I always make sure John, or the other guest, Andy, is also in the room."

With this, Lady Claire turned full onto Brenda's face to stare at her, not believing. She couldn't imagine that Brenda's statement could hold any truth. *Emma,* yes. Emma was the kind of woman with whom his lordship could love, with whom he could be comfortable. But Brenda? No. Impossible. Surely there was a place back in the States where Brenda would fit, but not here at the manor with Simon. Yet this was good fodder for gossip and she would encourage it. "I'm not surprised, my dear. I divorced him many years ago, and his womanizing was most of the reason." Anyone who knew Simon at all would never believe him capable of moral turpitude, but she knew that Miss Evans was too lacking in the power of discernment to grasp his sterling character.

"Was it?"

"Indeed. He approached a few of my friends; some found him too pleasing to resist. It was a topic of wide discussion until I had enough and decided not to live with him." She knew the lesson: send forth gossip about oneself, receive some back in spades. She had hit a mother lode.

If what Lady Claire said about Simon was true, then Brenda had to consider what she herself was lacking—Simon generally ignored her. She would have to think about that. Perhaps his remiss was due to Emma's interference. She dug for more slander to share. "I've had to lock my door at night. He came into my room before I had had a chance to learn about him, and he practically attacked me."

"No!"

"Yes. I'm sure you'll not repeat this. Fortunately, I screamed loud enough that Lady Joan appeared and scared him off." That was handy, Brenda thought, pulling out her frightful experience encountering Lady Joan in the hallway; just giving it a little twist.

Lady Claire wondered how many people Miss Evans would go to with this highly unlikely story. It was fortunate that Simon's character was unassailable by any who knew him, as well as to all who did not know him. And Lady Joan scaring Simon! About as likely as Lady Joan's acquiring corporeality.

"You had best leave there, my dear," Lady Claire said, using her advising face. The fewer women living at the manor, she thought, the easier it might be for herself to keep Simon company.

"Oh, I would love to leave, but you see, since Emma left suddenly without a word, even leaving behind some of her things, they insist on there being a mystery about her absence, and the staff and guests are under orders not to leave. The reason for her absence needs to be solved. I guess it's a situation where everyone is a suspect." Then she reached for a good stretch: "Simon could have done her in. Or even Andy."

Simon? That's about as likely as Mother Teresa doing away with the Pope, Lady Claire thought. Simon had a hard time killing ticks he found on Schrödinger.

For a few minutes they drove along in silence, mesmerized by the pile-up of outlandish lies.

"Who is Andy?" Lady Claire asked.

"He's Emma's old hiking buddy from when she was here in the fall on a tour. She's probably shagging both him and Simon." Brenda couldn't resist layering it on, for Lady Claire's stunned face took on a new dimension with each of Brenda's stories; inviting more.

"And what brings Andy to the manor?"

"Simon and Josh were hiking out to look for Emma, when they happened upon Andy. They invited him back to the manor."

Well! With this news about Ms. Chapman, Lady Claire knew her day would come when she could assure Simon that she had known all along that Ms. Chapman was unpredictable. After all—American? She would tell him how she had tried to protect him from the heartbreak of being close to Ms. Chapman. She had read the interloper's character, she would say. Simon would yet learn to trust her and let her into his life again. Ms. Chapman has somehow removed herself and she, Claire, would find a way to remove the other interloper sitting beside her.

Now they had reached Wickenbird Farm and the Mercedes turned into the drive.

"Larry, dear, knock and announce that we are here with two chairs."

"Certainly, milady." He shut the car's motor down and proceeded to the large farmhouse's front door. He knocked.

Both Lady Claire and Brenda watched him, thinking how smart he looked in his dark livery, sharp jaw, lean and erect. He reminded Brenda of the kind of man held high in her esteem, someone she wanted to meet; reminded Lady Claire of those wonderful men she had left back on the slopes of Davos. Well, she might get back there yet.

The door was opened by a woman whom Lady Claire and Brenda, caught up in admiring the chauffeur's form, hadn't noticed; hadn't much chance to see the woman for she ducked back into the house, apparently to call someone to deal with the chairs. Soon a man appeared at the door and gestured for the chauffer to drive around to the rear. A few minutes later Mars came out of the back of the house and looked into the car to see the chairs. Lady Claire rolled down the window.

"Hello," he said. "I am Mars Marsden. I cane the chairs. I see you have a pair of fine antiques. It'll be a pleasure to restore them."

"Willow only," she said. "These chairs are from the sixteenth-century and irreplaceable."

"Yes, ma'am." He didn't need to be told; he could see at a glance that the chairs were very old and fine. He knew as much about such things as the lady knew about hats. Larry opened the back hatch and went around to help Mars take out the chairs. "Excellent examples," he said to Lady Claire through the open window. "It'll be late winter, probably February before I'll have them ready."

"Do give them your top priority. My sunroom looks so bare without them," she said, presenting her sweetest smile. And as she handed him her card, she took a closer look at Mars—at his strong face, his searching eyes, and said with emphasis, "You can reach me here."

Then Emma came out the back door to see the chairs. She picked up one chair while Mars took the other, and together they crossed the yard and tucked the chairs into Mars' studio. Surely the eyes of the women waiting in the car were deceiving them. They watched the man and woman. Stared. Stared hard. Wasn't that Ms. Chapman? Truly looked like her. They watched Mars put his arm around the woman's shoulder as they walked back to the house. Then they saw him open the door for the woman and wait for her to enter. He seemed to have a special smile for her. The more they watched, the more they had a better view of the woman, and even after Larry had the Mercedes turned around and was headed out of the driveway, the more they knew—that that *was* Ms. Chapman. After Mars shut himself and Emma inside the house, Lady Claire and Brenda turned and gaped at each other with astounded, curious, questioning, gawks.

"So this is where she has got to," Lady Claire said.

Brenda was strangely quiet, but her worried demeanor would easily have passed for shock.

Well, well, Lady Claire thought. So the lovely Ms. Chapman, apple of Simon's eye, left because she has a new love interest. Wait until Simon hears. If he doesn't already know

With the chairs deposited at the farm, Claire was eager to get back to Cav Neumont Manor to tell Simon whom she had seen—*Emma at Wickenbird Farm*! Clear signs that she was there for an amour. That would teach Simon not to cast herself off so, to live in London when she had said she wanted to live with him again at the manor. She could barely sit still in the seat. Forgotten now Larry's lovely strong jaw. Forgotten now how statuesque he seemed in his uniform. *Simon. Just wait, Simon. Be there, Simon—not out somewhere.*

Brenda was completely speechless. She knew that she had left Emma dead. Truly dead. Not breathing. Not twitching. Lifeless. What had resurrected her? It was Emma she had seen. It was definitely Emma helping that farmer. What would happen now? Why was Emma at the farm? Did Lady Claire really know who she was? She appeared to know—but it was hard to tell, for Lady Claire was silent all the way back. Best thing to do now, Brenda thought, would be to keep her head down and wait.

When Hadley saw the Mercedes pull around the circle, he came down the steps to give a hand.

"Larry, wait here for me," Lady Claire said.

Hadley opened her door, and for once not thinking how she must look, Claire jumped out of the car and, brushing passed him, raced up the steps. "I must see Lord Haversham immediately," she shouted. Hadley dashed up the stairs behind her.

Brenda kept to a slow, uncertain pace as she came along behind. She would have hidden in her room, but the demanding need to know what Lady Claire was going to say to Simon, kept her downstairs to listen in.

"I'll tell Brooks you're here," Hadley said, showing the women into the drawing room. "I'm not certain his lordship is in."

"No! Summon his lordship immediately," Lady Claire said. "I'm sure he's in. I have something most urgent to tell him."

But Hadley knew the better judgment was to first tell Brooks, which he did, finding him in the pantry.

Even though the women had left for the day, Lord Haversham knew they would return. Oh, they would return, and in order to escape Miss Evans' aggressive, rude manners, and to give himself over to sadness, Lord Haversham had locked himself in his study, and now that's where Brooks found him.

"My Lord, Lady Claire is waiting in the drawing room for you."

Lord Haversham's breathing grew shallower; he had to work at taking a good breath. What now, he thought. It seemed he would never again have peace or a full heart. With eyes cast down on the page before him, he said, "Apologies, Brooks, but I'm not in for her."

"Sir . . . Hadley said that she sounded near hysterical, saying she had something most urgent to tell you."

Lord Haversham lifted his unhappy eyes up to Brooks. "Then, Brooks, I'll go down. Soothe the savage beast." And he slowly, and it seemed painfully, rose from his chair, adjusted his neck scarf and headed out of the room.

As he entered the drawing room, Brenda, her brain churning for ready explanations, had taken a seat and appeared calm. Claire was pacing—anxiously striding about from the window, where she would look out as though to find something startling, to the door where she expected Simon to enter. In two long strides, Claire covered the space to Simon, leaned right into his face, and pulled at his cravat as if to anchor him in place so he would concentrate on what she had to say.

"Simon. You will be astounded to know whom I have just seen. Out at Wickenbird Farm! MS. CHAPMAN! Your special friend! EMMA!"

Simon couldn't take in this news. It wouldn't register. He freed his cravat from her grasp and adjusted it. He had the usual look he carried these days of stunned disbelief.

"Simon! It's true! I saw Ms. Chapman at Wickenbird Farm. Wasn't that she, Brenda?" she looked to Brenda for support. Brenda gave the slightest of nods, not wanting to commit an opinion, uncertain, hoping by some miracle it had not been Emma.

"And to all appearances romantically involved with that cane-weaving farmer!" Claire added. Her eyes rolled to the ceiling and down. "Oh, he's attractive!" she nearly growled. "I can see the appeal."

Lord Haversham stared at Claire. Then he passed a severe glare from Claire to Miss Evans. He knew it couldn't be true. How could he dismiss these women now and try to find peace somewhere? Missing Emma, her absence, her unexplained absence, had made it a supreme effort for him to deal with others. He had kept up as much of an appearance for his guests—Andy, and Emma's son, Josh—as his drained system would allow, but trying to deal with Claire and the exasperating Miss Evans, was beyond his present energy level. "Claire, I know you mean well, but I'm sure you are mistaken; this is a cruel joke. Would you please excuse me, I'm not really feeling well." And, in truth, he was not well.

"Indeed, Simon, this is no joke. I saw Ms. Chapman, and she seemed to be helping the farmer . . . his name is Marsden. She helped him take my chairs into his studio. I saw her with my own eyes. Aren't I speaking the truth, Brenda?" Again she looked to Brenda for confirmation, and again Brenda barely responded.

"Did you speak to her?" he finally roused himself to play along.

"No, I was in the car. But I saw her come out of the house, help Mr. Marsden, then go back into the house with him. He had his arm around her. I'm obsessive about it's being Ms. Chapman. Both of us saw her." She looked to Brenda for a more vivid display of support and wondered why the woman seemed to be withholding.

Still incredulous, Lord Haversham could only think about getting Claire off on her way home, and Miss Evans off somewhere, and he didn't care where. "On you go, Claire. You will have to excuse me. I'll think about what you say, and about investigating. Ms. Chapman would not have left here without saying something. My dear, I assure you that Ms. Chapman's thoughtfulness and manners rival Debrett's." He left the room.

"You'll see, Simon," she called after him. She had no choice now but to leave. She turned to Brenda and ordered, "You must be my guest in London. I'll show you around." And behind her command was the desire to find out what would happen now at the manor.

Her anxious, eager desire to spread the news about whom she had seen, caused her to override the edges of protocol and on her way out she had to tell Brooks. "Brooks, I have seen Ms. Chapman. She's staying at Wickenbird Farm! You must convince his lordship. I had a good long look at her. I always knew there was something sneaky about that American. Classic."

As he showed her to the door, Brooks noted her gloating pose. He had seen that look on her many times. It was not within his realm for him to appear to hear, or to notice, and he kept a blank face, giving Lady Claire only a slight nod as he watched her driver open the car door for her. Then finally, as she again called out to him to convince his lordship of the truth of her words, he replied, "Yes, milady," and he turned away from the door, wondering exactly what he should do next. He was aware that his lordship had abruptly dismissed Lady Claire. Was aware that she was considered a potential nuisance, someone to be wary of, and that, as well, his lordship preferred these days to be left alone. Brooks knew his best move would be to say nothing. His lordship already knew what Lady Claire had to report. How valid was her news, he wondered. Of course, he knew about Ms. Chapman's sudden disappearance. Knew it was suspicious. Knew his lordship was very hurt as well as worried. And Ms. Chapman's son was here from America; worry bringing him here. Surely Ms. Chapman wouldn't have neglected to tell her son where she was. If she was at Wickenbird Farm, what would that mean?

After Brenda had said goodbye to Lady Claire, she escaped immediately to her room to think over what she had seen and what it could mean to her position at the manor. If Emma were alive, why didn't she return to the manor? Was Simon likely to go see whether that was Emma? And if it was Emma, what would she tell? Would she know what had hit her?

XVIII

The TV News Item

That same day a news item about the missing American woman, Ms. Emma Chapman, ran on the four o'clock news, and Sara, who often had the TV on while she worked in the kitchen, saw it, heard Trouvé's description, and saw her photo, as did Mars who had been nearby making a tea tray for Maida. He and Sara looked at each other with conflicted expressions; Trouvé belonged with the family now; they were hopeful it could work out that way.

Mars went up to Maida's room with the tray and the news, about which he couldn't decide whether to feel glad or sad. Maida had taken a seat at the window where she could look out onto the agreeable afternoon. Mars set the teacups and plates about, then took a seat at the table with her.

"Thank you, son. I especially enjoy my tea when you will sit awhile. You're awfully quiet and pensive."

Mars didn't reply, but followed his mother's gaze out the window.

"Who was in the big car earlier?" she asked.

"That was a woman from London dropping off two chairs." Then, after a pause, he said, "Something very important has just happened," but he didn't explain further, just continued to look out.

"Would you care to explain?"

In a way it seemed to him that this was the last of things familiar and beloved: the tea aroma that had seemed so steady, was now fleeting; the scent of fresh-cut grass wafting in the window, reaching in with the breeze—all so much a part of every day, now threatened to leave. Companionship. Nothing good could last long, he thought. Even the spring flowers were saying goodbye. Though he didn't want to give voice to it, he finally spoke, for Maida was waiting. "The authorities have just flashed on the telly, the photo of a missing woman, and have asked for any information about her." He couldn't go on directly, not wanting to face the idea that they could lose their unusual guest. That would be a great loss for them and especially for him. "There are many differences in the photo. I think it's old by a few years. Yet I have no doubt that it's Trouvé. Her name . . . is Emma Chapman."

Maida looked at him. She thought through every possible meaning that could entail. For a long silence, when even the spring afternoon seem to reach in to think about what that meant, Mars and Maida looked into each other's gaze.

"Did she see it?" Maida asked finally.

"No. She's in the study helping Jane with algebra. So pleased that she remembers numbers."

"What will you do about it?" Maida studied Mars, trying to divine his answer. He didn't answer. "She needs to know that they are looking for her," Maida said. "We've known all along that she must have family anxious for information about her. Of course we have to call the detectives."

"That's exactly what Trouvé has so far asked me not to do," Mars said. "Until she has complete recovery, she has fear for what happened to her. She almost dreads learning that unknown. She said she could remember everything since she woke in the bluebells. Everything as though since that time her senses were sharpened. And she knows that certain places, scents, and sounds hold meaning for her that will break through in time. I've asked Sara not to mention what we saw on the telly until I have a chance to tell Emma. Emma is surely her name. We must remember now to call her Emma." He struggled to cover his sad look.

Emma had told Hannah and Mars that she could smell bluebells, even detect the aroma of blue. And as she found her way to a road, halting and wondering whether she had been set down in a fairyland, her senses were heightened such that each leaf that fell, as it dropped from one shaft of air to another, had the sound of a piano being struck at random. She remembered the vivid scent of Harvey when he walked up to her as she leaned against the fence, and she could still recall the bassoon sounds that his tail played wagging through the air. And in her mind, she could still see Mars coming toward her, his clean scent pushing ahead in circles. She saw those circles: some traced a warm yellow, some blue. Those sharp oversensitive sensations had tapered to a thin waving line of memories that she could still detect. She almost knew who she was; it was just there lying underneath something, just there around the corner. Surely she would reach it anytime now; it felt so possible. But, her memories, such as they were, were encased in fear. Clearly, what had happened to her had not been normal, had in fact, been dire. And aside from going with Mars to the market, hoping some trigger there would help her to remember, she was frightened and had asked the family to be quiet about her presence until they could learn more.

Maida and Mars sat silent for a while thinking over what would be best to do. Maida had seen Mars' growing attachment to the woman they would now know as Emma. Could this be the woman she had hoped he would find? One just right for him? If she had anything to do with it, Emma would stay. Still, others may be hurting from Emma's absence.

"We know her family must be in despair wondering whether she's all right," Maida said.

"Right. I think about it every minute, every day."

Maida poured more tea for them while they dwelled on their bewildering thoughts and studied the world outside as though answers and happy solutions were waiting there. Mars had found new joy in Emma's presence; he knew, painfully, how he would feel should she leave, and that certainly, she must leave. And if she did would she be in danger? He wanted to protect her, keep her safely within the cocoon of the Marsden household. After a while Maida said, "You have to tell her."

"Indeed, I must. I'll certainly tell her as soon as she finishes with Jane. I feel that each minute I can put it off is one minute more that she is ours. I was about to go fetch her but the advert was over in a second. This will mean losing Emma, for surely the detectives will come for her."

With a heavy heart and feelings in turmoil, Mars came downstairs. Now was the time he had half wanted, half dreaded. They had learned something important that Emma needed to know, that he must tell her, and at once. He took each stair step as slowly as he could manage and still keep moving; each step a step closer to loss. Trouvé, whom they must begin to call Emma, had a history. Of course he knew that, but some part of him had been in denial—thought he might keep Trouvé at the farm forever. But her history would no doubt pull her away. He flip-flopped from the pleasure to bring joy to her and her loved ones, to the sad gap that would be left at the farm when she left: Trouvé, no longer working in the kitchen, no longer reading the paper by the fire, learning to make biscuits, taking walks with him in the evenings, sitting by while he caned. Always pleasant. And they had nursed her, helped her to recover, made sure she never over-tired herself, were ever watchful for her condition. He thought he had not before enjoyed a woman's company so much. Yet for days, along the periphery of his thoughts, had been the knowledge that her presence at the farm must be temporary, that the puzzle of her situation would resolve itself. And probably soon.

Now he reached the bottom stair and went with an unsteady tread down the hall to the study. As he entered the room, he heard Emma say, "In this case, two negatives make a positive." She turned from pointing to a line in the math book to look up and smile at Mars with her look that always said *I'm so happy to see you*.

But he remained serious. "I know two negatives that won't make a positive, at least not for me," he said, "that I need to discuss with you, Emma, as soon as you are finished with that."

It hadn't seemed strange to her that he had called her Emma. She nodded yes, and puzzled by his long face, watched him turn and leave the room. She continued the algebra lesson, giving it half her attention—the other half on something serious that Mars had in mind. What could it be? She knew it related to herself. Good news or bad? The only bad news he could give her was that she must leave Wickenbird Farm; surely that wasn't it. If she had to leave, she would miss the Marsdens and in particular, Mars; she had grown to care for him. And where would she go? If it were good news, what could it be? She knew, though, that it would be that they had found out where she belonged. A few inklings had been growing stronger for her the last few days. Her memory had been pulling more information from the universe. She knew it wouldn't be long now until she remembered everything.

She finished the algebra lesson, told Jane she was really coming along, learning it fast, would be ahead of her class if she kept working the way she was, then she went into the kitchen where Mars and Sara sat snapping beans. They stopped speaking when they heard her coming. Sara kept her head down, but Mars pulled out a chair for Emma. He forced a smile.

"Emma . . .," He had to firm his resolve. "We know who you are." The Earth stopped in its journey. It seemed that all motion was impeded. "Authorities are looking for you and have run a TV spot asking for information about you. You might reason, since I just called you that, that your name is Emma. *Emma Chapman*. They put up a photo and it is you. And I am happy and sad at the same time. Happy for you to reclaim your life, and sad that it will probably mean that you will leave us."

There was a long pause while Emma stood before them trying to hear, really hear, what Mars had said. *Emma*, so familiar, yet strange. Then "*Emma* . . ., I know that now. I know I am Emma Chapman." The crease down Emma's brow grew deeper. She sensed other memories trying to push through. Was this the good news? The look on Mars' and Sara's faces, trying though conflicted to look hopeful, didn't make it sound like good news. She waited for Mars to go on. Clearly he had more to say.

"I've written down the detective's number to call, but we wanted to let you know first, let you be the one to make the decision. There are people who are worried about you, looking for you, but we don't know whether you have something to fear from them. Perhaps talking to the detective will help you to know."

"I *do* have something to fear. Something happened to me; I think someone tried to kill me. I can't remember where, when, or why."

"I've thought the same, as well," Mars said.

"But, more often than not, I have a feeling of pleasant past situations," Emma continued. "Good feelings are returning. The cat I saw at the vet's brought back warm, good feelings. I keep seeing the name tag over his cage and I know it's very important for me. *Schrödinger*, a name I know so well. And I know that cat, and he knows me, but I just can't yet remember why. And yesterday, when that woman dropped off her two chairs, I caught a glimpse of her, and I know that face, an unpleasant memory actually, but not in itself evil. Then thinking about her face last night, I began to have more memories: I can almost remember a large building; it wants to come into my mind like a dream you wake up from trying not to let its features slip away." Her thoughts came rushing out needing expression. "And I have a recurring dream of looking down a long dark tunnel where at the end there is a man reaching out to me. I try to run to him through the tunnel, but every time it closes him off before I can get to him. Then, in that dark tunnel, I must walk back alone. And every time I see Maida's little clock, I remember something about a little clock I must have had. And I am close to people somewhere who care about me; just can't remember their names, or where they are. Where did I leave them? They must be so disappointed in me."

"When all is explained to them, Emma, they will understand. Have no fear about that. I hope very shortly you will remember everything, everything that happened to you. There has to be justice done on your behalf. You had a great shock from something. Something hurt you. I found you dazed, starved, and ill."

"We must call that detective," Emma said. "Please speak to him for me."

Mars had the number before him and he reached over for the phone and dialed. Emma heard a man's voice answer. She felt dread and expectation, and there was little hope for it but that two negatives—her being bludgeoned, and subsequently having amnesia—would fade away into something positive. It already had, she thought, as she looked at Mars' face.

"Detective Chief Inspector Adams, I'm Mars Marsden at Wickenbird Farm. We're certain we have your missing person, Emma Chapman. Would you kindly come out to the farm and speak to her?" He gave directions, then he hung up thinking this was the beginning of a sadness he would find hard to lift. He tossed one final bean into the pot, stood and went out the kitchen door so he could better control, unseen, the moisture that wanted to build up in his eyes. Emma began to snap beans as though this was normal; everything was normal, would continue to be normal. She and Sara didn't stir from the table—worked in silence until Jane, finished with homework, came into the room. Then Sara rose to set about cooking, wondering how many more meals, if any, they could
look forward to sharing with Emma.

DCI Adams and DS Sanders knocked. Emma and Mars and Hannah and Sara had been expecting them; had been sitting in the parlor, apprehensively formal, knitting their fingers together. Even Harvey sensed that something was up that required him to sit still and erect, and maintain his best behavior. Emma had arrived at Wickenbird Farm lost and ill, and now they knew the authorities were looking for a woman who looked like her. Emma felt peaceful and calm, for each had agreed that no matter what, she was not to leave with the detectives. Mars had heard their car pull into the drive, but he kept his seat, seemed frozen there. Twisted fate would intervene surely, and he wouldn't be required to go to the door, relinquish Emma, seal her fate, as well as his.

Then, the detectives knocked again and Mars rose to the dreaded unknown. He brought the detectives into the parlor and introduced them to Hannah and Sara and then said, "This is Emma Chapman." He felt ill at ease talking over Emma's head, but she had turned to stone, speechless. "Don't make any judgments until you've heard her story . . . as well as ours. She was struck by something, was badly injured, and has amnesia."

Emma wanted now with all her heart for nothing to happen, for nothing to change. Still she heard that ache: someone calling her, someone needing her. Even so, she felt the comfort of this place, something known and solid, this farm—chores required to be done here in peace—always in peace. She was needed here, and she needed to be here—a solid platform under her. One with love. Yes, love. She knew that. Had sensed it almost from day one.

"Ms. Emma Chapman? You look like Emma Chapman, although my photo is old," DCI Adams said with a questioning expression.

"It's feeling more like I am Emma," her hesitant reply. Then . . . "I am Emma," she said more firmly. She read the mixture of feelings on her friends' faces. They only wished her well; always that had been clear, topmost in their day-to-day caring. Then, quickly, as if she didn't say it quickly, she might never know how to, "And I know I am needed and missed by beloved people. In my dreams their faces are growing stronger. Time is bringing about my healing."

"Ms. Chapman . . . can you tell us what happened to you?"

"I don't know. Some accident. Something threatening . . . frightful. I remember waking in a field of bluebells, head throbbing, and then walking for days to find help and something familiar. Then Mars and his good dog, Harvey," she nodded to them, "found me down this road. I was exhausted and hungry and I don't think I could have walked another day. In fact, I had their farmhouse in view, but I wasn't sure I could make it here. These people have restored my health, took me to the doctor, helped me. Cared for me. Yet, I feel that someone somewhere, who wouldn't hurt me, needs me, and I must find out who it is." She saw conflict on Mars' face: hope, despair.

"Ms. Chapman, you have a son, Josh, an Aunt Ola, and someone quite worried about you, Lord Simon Haversham. They've all been frantically waiting for news about you."

The time had come full about, bringing memory, touching down on Emma, as she said their names. "Josh . . . Simon . . . Aunt Ola." Not a sound was heard through the long pause while Emma strained to look inward, then, "It's clear now. I can see their faces. How they must be worried." Memories were cascading in on top of each other. "And I had a contract with Greg. I had a job that I've neglected. I need to see and talk to my dear Josh and Simon and Aunt Ola. I need to explain to them. I need to explain to Greg." Her eyes searched wildly around the room as though she could summon them all immediately, not wait another second. Then her eyes grew still on Mars. "But I don't want to leave this family who've helped me so much . . . this peaceful, wonderful sanctuary. Oh, *what* can I do?"

That Emma had been found, and that she appeared to be safe and well, was possibly the greatest satisfaction DCI Adams had felt in his career. Yet, he knew that rushing her away from Wickenbird Farm would not be the best course. As well, Mr. Marsden had made it clear that when the detectives came to interview Emma, she was not to leave with them. And now that he saw she was being cared for in a good situation, DCI Adams agreed that that was the best decision. Move slowly. First he would let her family and Lord Haversham know that she had been found, and where she was, that she had been ill from malnutrition, but was well cared for, and was recovering from blows to the head. That she had had serious amnesia, and that she was recovering from that as well. Then he would arrange for them to come to Wickenbird Farm to meet her. Let them take it from there. He suggested this to the assembled people and each of them agreed that this was a safe plan. Besides, he underscored, something malevolent had happened to Emma, and no one, including Emma, had any idea what that had been.

"Right," Mars said. "When I found her, she had a nasty bruise on her face, and a bloody mess on her skull from blows to her head."

"Indeed," Hannah said, "that's how she arrived with us."

"But I need to speak with Josh and Aunt Ola and Simon on the phone now," Emma said.

"Let me tell them that we've found you and that you are quite safe and quite well, that you've had amnesia, but are recovering," DCI Adams said again. "I want to tell them privately, and then they can call you here. Until we know who attacked you . . . until you remember that . . . we must proceed slowly. We know it wasn't your son who, until recently, was in America, or your aunt, also there, and we checked on Andy Sullivan, a guest at the manor, and he hadn't arrived in the UK until two days after you went missing. And Lord Haversham's reputation is completely untainted; I'd personally vouch for his character. They're going to be ecstatic with the news; as it is, they are ill with worry. They've been searching all over for you, walking Neumont, walking Bingers." He stopped before telling her what they had found on Bingers, undecided whether it might be wise to first let her remember what had happened to her—and where. Much was still unknown. He didn't mention Miss Evans; let's see, he thought, whether Ms. Chapman, on her own, remembers Miss Evans.

On their way back to Cav Neumont, DCI Adams and DS Sanders discussed which step to take first. It was imperative to let Lord Haversham and Josh know immediately and let them phone Ms. Chapman and her aunt. "I think we should avoid Miss Evans if possible," DCI Adams said. "Her stories have always had an uncertain, mixed-up note, and we must include the possibility, as we have all along, that Ms. Chapman left their hike and was struck by a stranger. In which case why would her things be buried as they were? Times I wonder whether to release Miss Evans to go back to the States. She's truly an unwanted guest at the manor; his lordship has made that clear to us on a few occasions."

"Indeed he has," DS Sanders said. "It's easy to see that Miss Evans' testing, teasing, aggressive manner can't be pleasing to anyone."

"We must learn more though, before we release her," DCI Adams said. "And we must let Lord Haversham know right now before another minute passes. I just need a quiet minute to organize in my mind exactly what to say." He dialed the manor. "Brooks, kindly put his lordship on."

"Right away, sir."

The detective drummed his fingers, eager, but aware of pressing unknowns and concerns about the best way to arrive at the truth. "DCI Adams, speaking, sir. DS Sanders and I are on the road, but we had to speak with you immediately. Please keep this conversation private."

"Right. No one can hear me now."

126

"We've found Ms. Chapman." He wanted to rush and get it all out before Lord Haversham said anything. "She's very well, in good care now, but has been struggling with amnesia. Coming out of it, though, sir. Something most untoward has happened to her."

He waited now, but Lord Haversham, with all the consternation jockeying for place in his head, didn't know exactly what he had heard, or couldn't work his brain, or his tongue. He could only let a great gasp escape from his soul.

Since the news of Emma's whereabouts had been delivered fairly far already through the efforts of Lady Claire, his lordship's emotions couldn't settle on whether this was good news or bad. "Detective Chief Inspector Adams . . .," Lord Haversham had to force himself to breathe and find the strength to speak: say something, anything, "your call is timely, for my ex-wife has just told me she saw Ms. Chapman at Wickenbird Farm, and I've not known whether to believe it. I thought I must go out there."

"Rest assured, sir, it is Ms. Chapman. We've just had an interview with her and with the family, the Marsdens, who found her, and who have been caring for her. They've helped to restore her health after what appears to have been a severe blow to her head that caused her to have amnesia. They've even taken her to a doctor, and I assure you she's well, looks healthy, and as we talked to her, she is just now remembering you and Josh."

"A miracle." Lord Haversham could manage no more, kept wiping his eyes.

"She, of course, wanted to call you and Josh instantly, but I asked her to let me tell you first, and then have you phone her. I wanted to warn both of you to keep her situation private until we could learn what happened to her, but I see we've been too late with our caution, And, as I said, someone appears to have attacked her . . . strong blows to her face and head."

"I see. Horrible! Yes. Indeed, I'll tell Josh and give him your instruction. However . . .," he took a few seconds to think about what he wanted to say, "should I tell her employer? He's deeply concerned. And should Josh tell Emma's aunt? Also ill with worry?"

"Yes. Then you can arrange a visit with Ms. Chapman and the Marsdens. For several reasons no one thought it wise for me to bring her back to Cav Neumont just yet."

"Exactly. I completely understand."

XIX

The Meeting

Simon phoned Emma immediately. She was sitting by the phone. She finally knew herself and her situation completely, and every second she could almost hear the phone ring. She knew Simon would call as soon as he heard, as soon as he could get to the phone.

"Emma! Dearest, Emma!"

"Yes Simon, I'm here." Neither could find a way to continue. Time seemed suspended. There were no words important enough to express their loss, their hurt, their joy.

Then—, "Emma, I want to see you, hear your voice, hear what has happened. Are you all right?" His sentences cascaded over the phone in jerks, rushing and breaking like water over gullies. "Might Josh and I come there now?"

"Please come right away, Simon. We are expecting you. And, yes, I'm quite well."

He disconnected almost without saying goodbye, hard to say more with his voice trembling so.

"Mercy certainly fell like rain falling on all below," his lordship thought when the Morgan pulled up to the farmhouse.

"They're here, Emma," Mars said. "You go on to the door, and we'll wait to meet them after you. It's you they want to see."

Emma stood. She thought her heart would leap from her chest. Was this really happening? Would they be angry? How could they understand when she hardly did herself? She went to the door and without opening it, stood leaning her head against it. When finally, which seemed to be an eon, she heard the car's motor shut down, she opened the door slowly, afraid to look at the arrivals. Then she saw Simon step out of the Morgan; the sight of him felt like love, pure love. She knew him that instant, and wanted to fling herself through the air separating them. He knew his beloved Emma the moment she opened the door. It took all his patience to be still. He shut the car door, half-turning toward her, holding his breath. And when he saw her rush, spring out the door, he opened his arms. And like a child running, she almost knocked him over in her eagerness to hold him. Her heart warmed with the rush of his arms, his mouth, his voice. "I didn't want to leave you, you must know," she said.

"I never thought so. I believed something had happened to you, which made my pain even worse."

And they clung until Simon said, "My darling, there is someone with me who wants to give you a hug."

With her head buried in Simon's embrace, Emma had not seen Josh emerge from the Morgan. He had been waiting to see that it was indeed his mother who had sprung out the door. Now Emma looked around and seeing her son reached for him and wrapped him in her arms, tears streaming from their eyes. For a while no one spoke, a universe of words could not be found that could exist in this charged atmosphere. No one wanted to move.

Finally, Josh said, "Mom, are you all right?"

"Yes. Yes. These people have been so kind to me. Have helped me in every possible way. I love them, and you will also."

Simon wanted nothing more than to gaze at Emma with the incredible joy that they had found her, and to learn that she hadn't wanted to leave him. He could only say, "I've missed you, every day, every minute, every second. I've been sick with inexpressible worry and sadness. Emma, my love, it's wonderful to see you, to hold you. And I've wanted desperately to see Josh's joy finding you, knowing you are all right."

"And I," she said, "free of that pain by not remembering anything, was filled with a different pain for knowing something was terribly wrong, something vital missing." She broke off holding Josh, took the handkerchief that Simon had pressed to his eyes, and pressed it to her own eyes. Then, wordlessly, she took Josh's and Simon's hands and led them toward the house. "Come in now and meet the people who have given me a home when I was lost and knew not my own name." And she led them into the house and into the parlor where Hannah, and Mars and Sara and Harvey waited.

Anyone who knew Mars at all would see that the solemn smile he wore these days spoke of a dilemma he carried within, something inexpressibly conflicted. His awareness that he could not keep Emma, came to him as though he were required to live separately through each long moment.

As Emma led in Simon and Josh, Mars stood to welcome his visitors. Emma's introduction struggled to get out, her throat not yet loosened; still Lord Haversham extended his hand to Mars, and Emma said, "Lord Haversham . . . Mars. And, Mars, this is my son, Josh." The words "Lord Haversham" and "son" felt strange on her tongue, and had had to be pulled from a place far off.

"Your Lordship," Mars said, "please meet my sister, Hannah, and Sara, our housekeeper, who is really a member of our family. Both of them have cared for Emma when she was quite unable to help herself. And this is Harvey; he has cared as well."

Then remembering that tea might be helpful at this strange time, Sara said, "I'll bring in tea."

"And I'll be helping," Hannah said, and they left the room to fetch that good, welcome at all times, comfort.

Who should speak now, or what could he or she say? Each wanted to repeat the same statements of loss and gain and love. While thriving in the knowledge of Emma's welfare and in her joining her family, Mars was struggling to lift his soul from a certain sadness. He wanted to know just what was the connection between Emma and his lordship, but feared finding out. He hadn't stared from the window at the arrival, but despite his better self, he had caught a short glance and was witness to their clinging when they found each other.

Josh broke the silence: "Mom, I've let Aunt Ola know that we've found you, and you can imagine how happy that made her. She, like the rest of us, has been so concerned. Worried to death, and that includes Greg Tortle. He has called numerous times hoping something had been learned about your absence. Now all our hearts can rest."

"Oh, dear Aunt Ola. I'm so sorry," Emma said. "Please give her this number so that she can call me. And also, please give it to Greg."

"Indeed," Lord Haversham said. "Not one of our hearts has had a rest since you didn't return from that hike." He felt restrained in front of the Marsdens and Josh, but he wanted to squeeze Emma and not let go for a day, not until his arms fell off from tiredness.

"Was I on a hike?" Emma asked.

"Yes, you left with Miss Evans for a hike and she returned alone. She said you had left the hike suddenly to go to the village to buy a journal. But, of course, we checked with the stationer's, and you had not been in."

"Miss Evans?" Emma asked. She looked at Simon with the question as her brow pleated up.

"Right. Brenda Evans."

Emma waited for recognition. The name was familiar, but wouldn't come into focus. "Brenda," she said again. The name held a dark familiarity. "Brenda at the manor?"

"Yes."

"Yes, Brenda," she said finally. "I remember Brenda. I do not remember a hike, but certainly I woke in a field of bluebells, and had no idea how I got there."

Lord Haversham and Josh had agreed not to tell Emma at this time how Major had led them to her wallet and passport and mobile. There would be another better time to tell her that.

Sara and Hannah came in with a tea tray ladened with cakes and homemade bread and butter. A well of happiness seemed to have been newly plumbed in each of the household's souls, tainted perhaps by the dread that they would soon lose Emma to this Lord Haversham. They had not before met an earl, would have thought one to be either haughty, or eccentric to a shocking degree, or perhaps both, but this earl seemed easy and likeable. Grounded. And Emma's son seemed like one of their own—affable. But then he would have to be, wouldn't he? Being Emma's son and all.

Tea, the tongue loosener of all social devices, helped to generate the stories each held to illustrate his or her experience over the past month, and they each in turn wanted to tell his lordship what it was like finding Emma and living through her amnesia, and recovery. There was Mars explaining how they had some confusion when needing to refer to Emma with a name more personable than "Miss," and how they had decided to call her "Trouvé," for she had been "found." And now having to unlearn that and to learn "Emma." He had found a way to help them to laugh.

"Ah! If you're ever not yourself," Josh said, "we'll know you must be Trouvé, not Emma."

"Emma," Mars said. "A woman for all seasons under any name." He said it in such a way that his feelings for her vibrated around the room. "Emma has grown on us, become attached to us like bark to a tree. Losing her now, although I am happy she's finding her place, will be the same as losing my favorite cow." This did bring a laugh.

"Mars! How can you?" Hannah said.

"Surely Emma has learned that a farmer's most important assets are his cows," said Mars.

"Indeed, I feel honored," Emma said, and she gave Mars a smile of understanding.

Looking from Josh to Simon, she would not have been able to express her sense of loss and gain. But Simon did not look well. A cocoon of grief had its tight grip and seemed unable to completely release him.

Lord Haversham had many stories to tell about his past fears, his hope, and his new joy, and his stories piled up crowding out each other, until he finally found the coherence to say, "We'll take our leave now. Although we would love to take you with us, Emma,

DCI Adams has suggested that you not move to the manor until we know more about what happened to you."

"Yes. I agree," she said. "I have certain unknown fears about leaving, and for the time, I am safe here with the Marsdens. They've become family."

"We want you here, Emma, as long as we can keep you," Mars said.

"I know," she said.

When Lord Haversham saw the warm look Emma gave to Mars, he found that—mixed within his hopes—was a sense of anxiousness: now that he had found Emma, was she lost to him? With much hugging around, wiping eyes, and promises of gatherings to come, Lord Haversham and Josh said goodbye, but not before his lordship had said that, when it is decided prudent for Emma to return to the manor, all the Marsden household was invited as well.

At the car, though his intellect told him that now she would come back to him, Simon held Emma as if it were his last chance. After they finally said their goodbyes, and the Morgan was underway, he held her face in his vision until the farmhouse was beyond the bend.

Emma watched them drive down the road until out of sight. Then turning back into the house, the sad and bewildered look Mars wore as he held the door for her, was one she wore as well. That voice, Emma thought, the first thing about Simon she had loved. Loved without even knowing it was love. Then it was the sense of his strength. Then his character. Something she could rely on. And with all that she had found love when it was least expected. What was to happen next? Every day she was aware of Mars' growing affection for her. Mars. Dear Mars. Always kind. Never assuming. Always looking for ways to talk or walk with her. On some level she loved him, could live with him forever. They were so similar in character, helping each other. And there was Hannah, a potential sister; Hannah wanted her there. Emma felt that.

PART TWO

I

Waiting for Emma's Return

All the way home Lord Haversham had a sensation of floating. He couldn't think about anything but Emma. And now his thoughts, the atoms of his being, were soaring out over the fields. He could almost see them, so excited they couldn't be contained within his physical entity: had to, must, fly.

Now his atoms seemed to merge back into him, and he became grounded in present reality. "We still have serious concerns," he said, bringing Josh back to reality as well. "Obviously we must find out what danger your mother was in, and may be still. Someone wanted to harm her, perhaps wanted to kill her!" He shuddered as he said that. "If she comes back to the manor, she may be in danger." He didn't want to say it, but the name, Miss Brenda Evans, was surfing through his mind, wouldn't let go of him. "We'll have to continue to work with DCI Adams. He's the expert. We'll follow his guidance." Lord Haversham was talking aloud to himself. "He'll decide whether and when Emma can come back to us. Meanwhile, she seems to be in very good hands. How fortunate we are that Mr. Marsden found her."

Josh nodded agreement. "Right, sir. I can finally breathe deeply. I can't tell you how very happy I am. First losing my father and now possibly, Mom. And she's whole, hale, and hearty." He could relax for the first time in weeks. For the first time he could think about the future, make plans, enjoy something. He could now enjoy doing something.

"Quite. She is happy with them." As Lord Haversham said this he recognized a sad feeling invading his new found joy. Would Emma want to stay there? He hadn't declared himself to her in terms that carried a permanent message—that which he had acknowledged to himself. He wanted Emma permanently in his life, but hadn't quite been able to say it, unsure where she was in her universe. She worked; she liked her work. She lived mostly in New York. She liked being close to Josh, who was in college in Boston. And now that he knew where she was physically, where did she want to be? Then his thoughts ranged back to Miss Evans. What stance would DCI Adams take toward Miss Evans about allowing her to return to the States?

Lord Haversham took each step up and into the manor as though it were a bell tolling his joy, each one a different note, a different feeling: *Emma is okay, Emma hadn't wanted to leave.* The rain that had begun wouldn't dampen his enthusiasm and his brain was hot with plans; he projected one after another: holding Emma, tea or sherry with Emma, London with Emma, walking with Emma, dining, and more. He yearned for her. He saw them dining in the study that connected his room to hers, then he would pull her into his room for the night. He wanted to hold her night and day. He had waited long enough. He saw those events as clearly as he saw each separate raindrop in the slowing of time. He had dreams to savor—those from which he could safely awaken.

While Hadley took the car around, Brooks held the manor door open for Lord Haversham. He moved up the stairs more and more slowly and Josh took his arm to steady him; he thought he looked rather shaky.

"I'm right as rain, Josh. You go on into the library and have a sherry to celebrate. I'll be along shortly." Lord Haversham watched Josh as he eagerly bounded up the stairs taking them two together, but he, himself, didn't actually feel grounded. This must be how Lady Joan feels, he laughed to himself.

When Josh reached Brooks at the door, his excitement pushed out the eagerly awaited news, "Brooks, my mother is well, and she'll be back. She didn't want to leave us. Apparently, she was attacked by someone. We'll tell you more later."

"Yes, sir. Thank God for that, sir."

When Lord Haversham reached the top, he said, "Good evening, my good man, Brooks. I want to have a celebratory sherry in the library with Ms. Chapman's son. I'll lock the doors so Mr. Chapman and I won't be disturbed for this half hour. Then I want to ride out."

"Sir, I believe the rain looks determined to continue, such a threatening sky, and dark before its time."

"Right, and I thank you for your concern, but I won't be able to settle down yet. I need some activity to cool my brain, and Bud won't mind, he loves a gentle rain, and he has a warm stable to retire to after. Please have him brought round in half an hour."

"Yes, sir. I'll fetch a warm jacket for you."

"Brooks, you are ever always on top of things."

No sooner had Lord Haversham reached the library than Brenda approached—her cheerful attempt at normalcy firmly in place. "Please excuse us, Miss Evans," he said as he shut the door and pressed the lock. Then for the half-hour, he and Josh talked over their good fortune, their pure relief, pure and assuring as any rainbow.

Brenda had no idea where they had been, but she could guess—to see Emma. For the entire day, every voice around the manor had been silenced—mysteriously, she thought. Some were stilled because they knew what was going on, others because they wondered what was going on. Even Andy and John Britely had little to say to Brenda, but she was determined to hang on. Wait it out. Act normal. Nothing to fear. She phoned Lady Claire to discuss the situation.

"I feel certain that Simon and Josh went out to the farm today, and met the woman we think is Emma. Everyone is being very quiet. Secretive. No one will tell me anything, Josh and Simon have shut themselves in the library."

"Ah, he's probably ashamed that he had so much faith in Ms. Chapman. Ashamed to show his face. The future looks quite interesting. Hang in there," Lady Claire said, knowing that Brenda's hanging around would only inflame Simon. Would he now arrange to move her out?

"Maybe things will settle down soon. I prefer it here without Emma. I want more time with Simon."

"Even though he has been a bother, my dear?" Lady Claire said, forming it into a warning.

"Certainly. He needs to be taught a lesson. I well know how to do that." Lady Claire was useful, Brenda thought, but she could be taught a lesson as well, and that was not to try to chase off Brenda. After disconnecting, Brenda went to the drawing room to join Andy and John for sherry, but the moment she had filled her glass, and pulled a seat over near the men hoping to engage them in a bit of gossip, Brooks came in.

"His lordship has asked me to tell you that he won't be joining you until dinner. He's about to take a ride out."

Questions spread across the men's faces; they swapped glances. They had been told earlier that his lordship was driving out, perhaps to find Emma, but they had been requested to keep it quiet, and they had been expecting a word from Sir Simon.

Before his lordship could leave for his ride, he answered his phone. It was. It was Lady Claire.

"I told you Emma was out there," Claire said.

"I can't deny it, Claire."

"And, for all appearances, she has found a love interest."

"You must not repeat that, Claire. You don't know the facts. Josh and I have been there and talked to Emma, heard what happened first-hand."

"So you say. What *is* the story, if it isn't an international secret? Classified? Everyone's been so hush-hush. Even Brenda won't say. I asked her why did Emma leave, and her tongue was tied, not like that motor-mouth at all."

"I can't discuss it, Claire. Perhaps in time . . .,"

"I know that detectives have been at the manor. In fact, Brenda revealed that early on, on our trip out to Wethermere with the chairs. I know," she continued, irreverently guessing, "Emma stole the little gold clock, and you called in detectives, Emma confessed, and she's in a detention center that Farmer Marsden runs at the farm." She laughed.

"Claire, you should turn your hand to fiction." Lord Haversham did not wish to give Claire more of his time. He found himself fighting off weakness; moving felt like slugging through clay. "I really must hang up Claire; some business here is pressing. Ta," and he disconnected.

Though Brenda and Lady Mardling were drying up as news sources, Lady Claire knew all would be revealed in time. Simon likely was reluctant to admit that the lovely Emma was finding fulfilment elsewhere. When Farmer Marsden calls her in winter to come pick up the finished chairs, she might learn at that time that Emma and he are joined in holy matrimony. Stranger things had happened. Meanwhile, she would find additional reasons to keep visiting the manor, even with Peter at college she intended to be in on first-hand knowledge.

"Sir," Brooks said, he had come in to the library with a warm jacket for his lordship. "Hadley has Bud ready to go." Lord Haversham didn't look eager; clearly, he wasn't well, should not be exposed to the rain. "And the heavens are about to drop, sir. A downpour is likely."

Lord Haversham drained his glass, and after letting Brooks help him on with the jacket, and thanking him, said, "Though, I must take a ride. My tension needs a soothing workout. Just a short one. Major, you wait by the fire. No point in your coming in with a wet coat. Josh, if you want to join me, Hadley will bring around Maggie for you."

"No thank you, sir. I'm content to wait here by the fire as well."

"Then I'll join you at dinner." He reached down to stroke Schrödinger, who knowing something important had happened, had also not been able to settle. He had looked for his lordship and followed him when he could. "Schrödinger, my pal, our friend Emma will be back among us, and not too long from now . . . if we're lucky." As Simon stood to leave, for a few seconds he was unsteady.

At the door Brooks handed him a cap. "Not now, thank you, Brooks. It sounds like a gentle rain and I need to feel it washing over my soul, clearing away the sludge of fear pressing me down the past weeks. Cool my brain."

Brooks, cap in hand, focused on Lord Haversham a concerned frown that his lordship preferred not to see.

Not wanting to keep his guests waiting for dinner, Lord Haversham did not ride far, or long, merely half way to the village. The cool, light rain washed down his head and face and into his collar, but despite that, he felt warm and soothed, even rewarded: perhaps rewarded more than he deserved; rewarded for never giving up, never suspecting Emma. Sometimes, however, wondering whether Miss Evans' stories could contain any germ of truth. Again, time seemed to slow and he felt each raindrop separately, heard its unique sound separately from its brethren.

Back at the manor, when he turned Bud over to Hadley, his lordship was thoroughly soaked, but the fire in his brain had cooled some. Again he was slow going as he took the stairs to his room to change for dinner, each step an effort. With Pearce, his valet's help, he discarded wet clothes. He did not really feel like eating, his heart seemed cordoned off into both joy and exhaustion, but he had guests who were waiting for him, eager to share in the good news, and he wouldn't disappoint. Despite efforts to keep mum about Emma and her situation, he sensed that the news was out by way of the usual webs dancing about like static electricity. So, dressed in a dry suit, he joined the others in the drawing room, and when the gong rang for dinner, he made it into the dining room. He would not lead in Brenda and that effort was left to Andy.

At dinner, after the commotion of passing and filling dishes had been finished, and each had settled into serious dining, Andy said, "Thank God, Sir Simon, you found Emma to be okay and in good health. It'll be good to see her again. When will she come here? Can you tell us what has happened to her?"

Brenda was silent. She had already offered praise for Emma's recovery and now she composed an offhand look as though it were all beneath her notice. She felt that she should offer something such as *Oh, it will be a fine thing to see Emma*, but it was hard to override the lump in her throat caused by uncertainty, and perhaps a bit of fear.

Lord Haversham noticed that she seemed unable to eat—played with her food. Well, at least that way, she won't be waving around her fork in that ghastly manner, he thought.

No one replied to Andy, and finally, his lordship said, "My head is too full now, Andy. I'll tell you about her travails tomorrow. Let me just say for now, she did not want to leave Cav Neumont Manor; she met with some kind of accident, was quite ill and is now healed. She should be back with us soon."

Although Lord Haversham didn't wish to have coffee, he was unwilling yet to yield to his tiredness and he suggested the company adjourn to the drawing room for coffee. As Brooks entered with the coffee tray, Brenda, who had already found the closest seat near Simon's, jumped up. "Simon, you are tired, let me pour for you."

But Brooks having barely set down the tray, and ever wishing to intervene between his lordship and this woman who seemed like a vulture on watch, rattled a cup into a saucer, grabbed the pot, and said, "Miss Evans, I've got it." Then he handed his lordship coffee. Simon had barely time to take a sip and look around to see that John and Andy and Josh and Brenda were all served, when Hadley came in with the phone.

"Your Lordship, you have a call and I know you don't wish to take it now, but the gentleman said it is urgent."

"Thank you, Hadley. Excuse me please," he said to the group. "Let me hear what this is about and I'll tell whoever it is to phone again in the morning."

As Lord Haversham said hello into the phone, the group waited silently, not wanting to interfere with his lordship's call. It seemed ages that he listened to the caller. Then while he continued to listen, he stood and walked the phone to the back of the long room. "I see, I see." He said nothing more for another long pause. Then, "I'll inquire. Thank you for this information. Let me have your number, so I can let you know. But it will be tomorrow, probably." He disconnected the phone, handed it to Hadley, then came back to his seat. As he attempted to join in a conversation again with the group, he had to work to act as though he had heard nothing unusual in the phone call, but he wanted to study Miss Evans. He made a calculated guess that, based on Miss Evans' usual actions,

142

she would attempt to be the last one to leave for bed, hoping to have private time with him. Though he was so exhausted, he would wait. He wanted a word with her.

His wait was rewarded, for shortly, one by one the men said goodnight and took their leave. As Simon and Brenda sat there alone, he wished he could physically somehow remove the proud aspect of her face. He understood that she thought she had won something; the last intention he meant for her to have. She refilled his cup and gave him a warm, understanding, but misguided, smile. "Ah, Simon, it's nice to have a private moment with you. I've waited. I know that lately you've had much to deal with." He cleared his throat. "Miss Evans . . ."

"Oh, Simon, do please call me Brenda," she cut in."

"Miss Evans, have you been taking your medication?" And he looked at her from up under his lowered brow. "That phone call was from your gentleman friend, Luke Williams."

"Medication? Luke? I don't understand." She was prepared for this.

"Mr. Williams is quite concerned about your keeping on your medication regularly; concerned enough to reach me about it after many failed attempts to get assurance from you."

"I really don't understand why Luke would call, or worry about, as you say, my medication. I'm not on medication." Her look of innocence would have fooled most, but not Lord Haversham. It was true that for the past two weeks Luke, calling Brenda on her mobile phone, tried to get assurance from her that she kept up with her medicine. Brenda wanted to convince him that she was quite healthy and didn't need the anti-psychotic drug. Luke knew better, the memory much alive of her going for him with a knife. Finally, Brenda had stopped answering his calls. Now that he had caught up to Lord Haversham, he was anxious to give him the news about Brenda's illness, and about her hospitalization, and that her doctor prescribed medication that she must stay on in order to avoid possible psychotic episodes.

"Luke is merely trying to poison my opportunities," Brenda said. "He has been after me for weeks, and can't adjust to my rejecting his attentions."

The fire was returning to Lord Haversham's brain, and before his eyes, images seemed to wave, and he felt his strength slipping further away. Yet he wanted to confront Miss Evans on this issue—as hard as it was for him to endure being up one more minute. "Miss Evans, in the light of the story you've been telling us all along, that Mr. Williams was enamored with Ms. Chapman, and that he had been calling *her*, and that she had made a commitment to him, I can hardly accept that now . . . you were the one he wanted all along."

"Oh, it's true, Simon," thinking quickly—Brenda prided herself on her persuasion skills, and she had had days to practice her ongoing themes. "You see, when I rejected Luke, he switched his attentions to Emma." She tilted her head back at just such an angle to support her teasing, self-assured expression, as though her statements were unassailable.

Sir Simon's amazement at her gall was outweighed by his extreme tiredness. He set down his cup and saucer, stood slowly, and as he left her sitting there, he said, "I must retire. We'll talk about this again tomorrow. Meanwhile, take your medication, Miss Evans."

But on the morrow, he couldn't tell anyone anything, couldn't phone anyone, couldn't warn anyone that Brenda could become psychotic; he was overtaken by fever and was completely delirious. He didn't leave his bed. John called a London physician, Dr. Smythe.

II

Safe at Wickenbird Farm

"**M**om, Simon did not come down for breakfast, and Brooks told us that he was ill."

"Oh dear," Emma said. She spoke to Josh over the phone. "What's wrong with him?"

"We don't know. But it's easy to guess that it's from exposure and the long strain of worry. Several times he walked about or rode out on Bud in chilly rain and came in fairly soaked. And coupled to that, his stress over your absence wearing him down . . . not knowing whether you were okay."

"I don't know what to say. Poor Simon. I know him to be strong and vital. I'm so sorry to have caused him grief. I need to see him. I need to be there. I'll ask Mars whether he can have a chance to drive me to the bus."

"Bad idea at this time, Mom. DCI Adams asked you to stay there for good reason. Some harm befell you, and he needs to find out what happened, or you need to remember it, if you can. Stay put until he gives the okay. I'm serious. Simon wouldn't want you to take a chance either. I'll be out to see you this afternoon. Mr. Britely is letting me use the Morgan."

"Josh, please say hello to him for me."

That afternoon when Josh arrived at Wickenbird Farm, Emma began to make tea for him until Sara intervened and sent her and Josh along to the study. "I'll bring your tea. You need privacy. You've both been through so much, and it's time you had a private talk together."

But before Emma and Josh could talk about the small, daily, normal issues life presented, now that Emma's crisis was over, and Josh could relax with relief, he had to first give her the bad news: before he left the manor, Brooks had said that Simon was not responding, seemed to be delirious, and Brooks had called the doctor. "I'm eager to hear the doctor's report," Josh said. "I dreaded to give you this news, but you had to know."

"I really must go there! I'll go back with you," she said. The peace and security that Emma had enjoyed during the past weeks in the Marsden's' care began to fail her. The bond she had uncovered, remembered, between Simon and herself was threatened now—just when she had yearned to relive it.

"No!" he said, fixing her with firm assurance. "I can't take you with me. When DCI Adams gives the okay, someone will come for you. I promise I'll call the detective on my return, or tomorrow, if it's too late tonight, and plead on your behalf. Otherwise neither you nor I can be responsible for your welfare." Josh stared his mother down and spoke with his sternest voice. She might still be in danger; he remembered her wallet and other items that were found in a hole in the bluebells. Who attempted to bury those? And why? His mother had not been told about that.

"Then please let me know what he says, as soon as you know. Tell him it's vital that I help Simon. And Josh, I could use my laptop. Would you bring it to me? It should be in my room at the manor. Also, my cell phone. As it is, I have no way to pay for your college expenses, or for my own, and I want to repay the expenses I've incurred for the Marsdens." Recently these fine details had been trickling into Emma's memory; everyday chores and responsibilities vying for attention. The day before, during her

146

phone call from her Aunt Ola, after all expressions of love and gratefulness for Emma's safety had been uttered, Ola assured Emma that she had covered Josh's expenses, and Josh had collected Emma's bills and they had as well been paid. "Not to worry," Ola had said, "you can repay me next year, or anytime when you are back." Concerned about the accident and subsequent stress, everyone took steps to guard Emma from further worry.

"I'll find your laptop and have someone bring it out for you." Josh omitted mentioning her phone; soon enough she would learn where it had been found. "Now that I know you are okay; I have to return to college. I'll be leaving day after tomorrow, and I hope to see that Simon is recovering before I leave."

So, that evening, when Josh arrived back at the manor, he asked John Britely for DCI Adam's number, and phoned him. "My mother is pressing me on two points," he said to the detective. "She wants her laptop, and I looked in her room and it isn't there. More pressing is that she is anxious to be with Lord Haversham. They were very close, you know. It might be good for him to see her."

"Not yet," DCI Adams said. "Your mother is safe at the farm, and that's the most I can say right now. I'm concerned about Miss Evans; apparently, she should be on medication to prevent possible psychotic episodes. I don't want your mother exposed to her until I find out more. I just today had a phone conversation with Luke Williams in New York. He is, or was, Miss Evans' colleague and live-in partner. He's been trying to reach her, but she wouldn't take his calls, and so he tried to reach your mother." Josh could hear what sounded like the detective banging a pencil on his desk. "When that failed," DCI Adams said, "he phoned the manor. But when his lordship didn't return Mr. Williams' call this morning as promised, Mr. Britely suggested that Mr. Williams call me. And he did. He explained to me that Miss Evans should be on medication, and he didn't think she was. You can be sure that caught my attention!"

The pencil banging continued, punching out each of the detective's words. "Medication!" he said. "Medication important enough for Mr. Williams to call all around the world to be sure she is taking it! So I asked him to tell me about it." The detective paused to think which part came first. Then he laid it all out for Josh: "He told me that Miss Evans' behavior could be unreliable. Indeed . . . when off her medicine she became deeply depressed, anxious, and obsessive compulsive. And that one night she had flown into a rage over a burned dinner and had attacked him with a knife." Ouch, Josh thought, they all, everyone at the manor, could be in danger. On occasion Brenda did seem to be manic. He waited for DCI Adams to go on.

"That was why your mother covered for Miss Evans in New York when she took sick leave this past fall. Mr. Williams had had to restrain Miss Evans and call 911. She was taken to hospital for treatment and evaluation by her physician, possibly to adjust her medication. Turned out that Miss Evans told her doctor she had felt so good the past few weeks living with Mr. Williams, that she had quit the medication, certain that she didn't need it. Back on the anti-psychotic drug and back at work, Mr. Williams said she seemed quite adjusted, well, and normal. But, no one knows what she did after arriving at the manor. We don't know whether she was involved in your mother's accident. It's not enough to just suspect her, and your mother can't remember what happened on that hike. She could have left the hike and been attacked somewhere else. Miss Evans' story is that they hiked on Neumont, and not on Bingers. Even so, your mother's personal things were found on Bingers."

"I see," Josh said. "Scary situation. Everyone at the manor tries to avoid Brenda. Bad vibes there that no one understands."

"I'll be out to the manor soon to question her again," DCI Adams said, "now that I know more about her illness. Meanwhile, watch your back."

"Sir, before I let you go, Mom has asked me to bring her cell phone and wallet. What shall I say? I understand that she was to slowly be filled in on the bad news, because the fact that her things were buried does appear that there is someone out there who will harm her. I can't imagine that she would have purposely dumped them." Josh waited through a long pencil-thumping space for a reply.

"I knew she would be wondering about her mobile and wallet. I'll take them to her, and tell her where we found them. It's probably just as harmful to let her think we're hiding something from her, as it will be to tell her everything we know, which isn't much. You might tell her that we have her mobile, but don't mention the computer yet . . . we haven't found it."

III

Telling Emma

Early the next morning DCI Adams and DS Sanders called on Emma at Wickenbird Farm. They had called ahead and Sara greeted them with fresh hot biscuits, honey from the farm's hives, and coffee. Mars and Hannah joined Emma and the detectives briefly, then excused themselves, for they would leave the detectives to talk to Emma privately. But before they even half rose from their seats, DCI Adams asked them to please stay, if they could. It would be okay for all to hear what he had come to tell Emma. The pain pressing Emma's face warned DCI Adams that she might be expecting bad news; he wanted to reassure her. So he quickly said, "Ms. Chapman, we've come expressly to give you your personal things, and to tell you where we found them . . . aside from your computer that is, which we haven't found." He handed her a parcel from which she removed her wallet, passport and cell phone. She thumbed through the wallet looking at the photos of Josh and Aunt Ola.

"Now I really feel like Emma." Her brow relaxed some, a small smile stating itself again on her pretty face; *he hadn't come to warn her that Simon was worse.* Next to the good health of her loved ones—and that now included the Marsdens and household, and in particular Aunt Ola and Josh, and very much in particular Simon—all else were trifles. She looked at DCI Adams with a more at ease, expectant expression.

He thought he might as well get right to the point. "You remember waking in a field of bluebells . . . Lord Haversham and your son found your passport, mobile, and wallet buried in that bluebell field. He waited five seconds, then said, "But no laptop."

Emma's eyes searched off into space. Why would she have left them? They should have been in her waist pack. She waited for DCI Adams to go on.

"Someone had attempted to bury them forever out of sight, dug a hole, and covered them up in an area off the trail where no one would *ever* tread. Had it not been for Lord Haversham's dog, Major, your things might have rotted into the ages. That's why we want you to stay here until we learn who tried to hide them."

"I see. Of course it would help if I could remember that day, that hike. I do remember now that Brenda wanted to hike Bingers, and I also remember telling her that it would be difficult going. Perhaps the rest will come to me soon; more memories arrive each day. So far, I just remember walking along, then nothing . . . until I woke up alone."

"And she says you hiked Neumont, not Bingers."

"Well, I do clearly recall now that it was she who requested Bingers. To see the bluebells."

DCI Adams jotted something in his notebook. He then remembered Miss Evans' alleged problem. "Do you remember anything about Miss Evans taking medication? And do you know why she took sick leave when you covered for her?"

"No. I know nothing about any of that. I wasn't privy to her medical situation." Emma paused to think over the next puzzle, then said: "I wonder where my laptop is."

After the detectives left, Mars asked Emma to take a walk with him and Harvey. Harvey, until his leg solidly healed, was still on a lead, and someone would take him out to walk several times a day. As they walked, Mars wanted to look at how pretty Emma looked in the dress she had bought in Cav Neumont. He found he had to tell her: "That dress suits you. You're very graceful in it. And in your new shoes, as well. I think I enjoy taking you to evensong just to see you in those clothes." Maybe he had said too much, he thought, and he said no more.

"Thank you. I wanted to save them for when I get to see . . .," She stopped—not wanting to tread on the feelings that Mars appeared to have developed for her. Her feelings for him had grown as well. The truth was though, since remembering who she was and where she belonged, she had not stopped thinking about Simon—day or night his was the voice calling for her. She belonged with Simon. And now he was ill and she couldn't get to him.

"See Lord Haversham." Mars finished her sentence. "I do understand. You must leave us, and probably soon. It will be our loss. We're all agreed to that."

"If I do get to go back to the manor, it won't be the last time I'll visit with all of you, if you'll still have me. I love your farm and your family." She took a quick, shy glance up at Mars. She loved him too, in a sense, but it wasn't wise to say so. "If you would have me, I would come here for a visit every year." Then dreaming ahead, she added, "Perhaps both Josh and I could help for a week or two during your busiest season. I love Maida and I enjoy reading to her, and I enjoy helping you at the market, seeing all the people. And perhaps next time I can make change more quickly. I was surprised at how easily I remembered how to solve quadratic equations when I began to help Jane with her homework."

As they turned back toward the farmhouse, Mars thought if that would be the best he could have of Emma's company, he would have to be grateful for that.

IV

Brenda Questioned Again

When DCI Adams interviewed Brenda again, he did not say that he knew Emma was at Wickenbird Farm, or that Emma's wallet and such had been found on Bingers. But still he had little to go on.

No one had given Brenda information, however, the nearly silent buzz around the manor, and the celebratory mood that she saw in the men—except for Simon who stayed in his room—gave her plenty of reason to believe that they—Simon, and perhaps Josh—had seen Emma. So Brenda's story took on even more emphatic remembrance with detailed descriptions of what Emma had said, how she had walked off, and that she had disappeared. She remained stalwart against DCI Adams' relentless badgering about medication. No, she maintained. She had not been on any, wasn't supposed to take any meds. She couldn't imagine why Luke was mixed up about that. Where did he get that hare-brained idea? Now Brenda's confidence had matured into solid expectations of a life with Simon, a life at the manor. She deserved that, she thought. It must be true that Emma *was* at Wickenbird

Farm: hadn't she seen her there? Apparently Emma wanted to stay there, and didn't know that she had attacked her and left her for dead. Well, as long as she stayed there, she wouldn't be interfering in Brenda's life.

Lord Haversham's fever was not responding to treatment; in fact, he seemed to be worse. Everyone at the manor walked around in mournful silence, unable to think about much else. Dr. Wisely from the Cav Neumont Clinic came every morning, and a nurse came morning and evening. Brooks and Mrs. Penrose and Pearce, and even John Britely took turns keeping cold packs on his lordship's brow and sponging his arms with cool water. Between the efforts of the physician and nurse, an IV was kept going to administer essential fluids. Finally, Brooks was constrained to tell Lady Mardling, Lady Southway, and Sophia that his lordship was ill and that the doctor was in attendance, etcetera, etcetera. And although cook produced tasty dishes to keep everyone going, the esteemed Ladies wanted to contribute, and nearly each day they would arrive with pâtés, cakes, and pies.

Afternoon teas, not joyful by any means, were yet companionable and succoring as all gathered in the drawing room to commiserate over the offerings and think about his lordship. Commune in their own silent way, prayerfully. A source of consternation, especially for the doctor and any others attending, was that in instants of near lucidity, Lord Haversham called for Emma: a plaintive, doleful cry that broke the hearts of those within hearing. It would help, they thought, if Emma were here. Definitely help. Eventually John Britely urged DCI Adams to consider bringing Emma back to the manor.

"His lordship calls and calls for Ms. Chapman. I know you recommend she stay on the farm, and certainly your advice is well taken, but what if, Heaven forbid, Sir Simon doesn't recover?"

DCI Adams and John Britely took a moment to think about that: *Simon and Emma not to see each other again!*

"Let me think about that," DCO Adams said, "and come up with a plan. If we can protect her. We're not sure . . .," he broke off, then, "I'll ring you."

Although Brenda was not shut out of the drawing room teas, she was shut out of the hearts and minds of the attendees who universally felt that her presence had about it something foreboding. And only Lady Claire had taken steps for her own illicit purposes to cultivate Brenda's friendship. Brooks and John Britely both discouraged Lady Claire's visits, saying that the doctor wouldn't permit his lordship to have visitors. And anyway, it wasn't in Lady Claire's nature to worry much about Lord Haversham's outcome. She would push his illness to the far dark corners of her mind, but it would inevitably move itself to the light forefront with the consideration that he carried a large insurance policy in her name. Because of Peter, he would assure that she was taken care of. Her blithe spirit was not easily dampened by Simon's condition.

Brenda, certain that Simon would like her presence in the sick room would make her way to his room almost daily, determined to gain entry. And each time, as she neared his door, Lady Joan would appear at a warning distance down the hall. There she would make ominous sounds and glare at Brenda, until Brenda, hair rising on her arms, would give up, saying to herself—it wasn't worth it—she would try again the next day. Sometimes—although she could usually ward it off—an image of Emma's wallet and other items that she had buried would appear before her eyes. When this happened, she couldn't immediately push the image away. Even if she closed her eyes, she would see Emma's passport, or cell phone, or wallet. At first, because she was so sure of the stories she had built, this happened rarely, but these days this image was appearing with increasing frequency. Was the image trying to tell her she was suspected in the crime? Well, if so, there was no proof that she had something to do with burying them, or that she was ever on Bingers. She had to keep reminding herself.

V

Emma Remembers the Hike

Sometimes on a raw, chilly day, Mars would take a few hours in the studio to work on caning, and on this day, although he had a good wood fire there to warm body and spirit, Emma knew he would like a cup of tea. She took a tray out to him.

"Thank you, Emma. Perhaps you can sit here and keep me company whilst I work on this chair."

"Yes, sitting a spell will be nice, and I can monitor all your mistakes," she laughed.

Mars looked up at her—it wasn't easy to get a laugh from her, with Lord Haversham reported to be so ill. "I've made a few on this one," he said. "It's a little devil. So dried out, even in this humid weather. Probably sat right by a heater for most of its life. But look at its beautiful lines. Someone spent some time bending this wood." He drew his hand down the chair's supports to show Emma what he meant.

Emma nodded, and while she watched Mars, and let her eyes follow the threading in and out as he wove the previously softened rattan, she thought about life weaving in and out, connecting her to Mars and Simon. Weaving in. Weaving out. Connecting her to Greg Tortle. Connecting her to Brenda. Connections that wove together like vines that turned together among themselves. Downed leaves weaving into a carpet. Bluebells. A weave of blue. Hiking. A weave of hiking along Bingers. She remembered hiking. With Brenda. Brenda had wanted to hike Bingers and so they left from the south wing. In her mind she could see the south hallway and how it looked before they left. There was the large Chinese urn that held hiking sticks. They had each taken one. She wore the waist pack that she had on when Mars found her. Then she remembered that she had put into it her mobile phone, wallet, and passport. Why? Because she didn't go anywhere without them, and so they were always in the waist pack when she was out and about. Someone had to have removed them.

"My, you are far away," Mars said.

"Yes, I have been remembering more details from before you found me. I guess your soothing, rhythmic work, the warm fire and good tea, has opened up a window of memory previously shut. I have something important to tell DCI Adams."

"Ah, in that case, I welcome you always to join me whilst I work; every detail remembered will be progress."

"Mars. Dear Mars. I would love to, but I think my small contribution in the house is also worthwhile. Earn my keep, you know. Speaking of earning my keep, I need to ask DCI Adams when I can return to work. I had a contract in London, you know. And if it has started, Greg, no doubt, needs my assistance."

"Yes. I do know. I don't like to think of your going off to London, but I know you have expenses.

"Let's go in, Emma, I have chores in the house, and it's shortly time for us to join the others for a sherry. I want to take one up to Mum, as well. And then see what I can do in the kitchen to help Sara."

"And I want to phone DCI Adams," Emma said.

VI

Simon Desperately Needs Emma

"Lord Haversham is not improving." Dr. Wisely at the manor spoke to Dr. Smythe in London. "And he keeps whispering 'Emma'. I think we must bring her to his lordship, if only for a day. In his condition I'm not even sure he remembers that she has been found and is okay. Her presence may encourage him to conquer this fever. Might I speak to DCI Adams about that? I'm quite concerned; his lordship is deteriorating."

"Right. By all means then, have a word with him, and do catch me up with his decision."

As soon as Dr. Wisely disconnected the call with Dr. Smythe, he dialed, and reached DCI Adams. He gave the detective the same information about Lord Haversham as he had given Dr. Smythe, adding: "I fear his lordship might not rally, sir."

"Then, we must bring in Ms. Chapman for several reasons. It might help his lordship to know she is there, and she probably wouldn't forgive us if we do not. So be it. But I don't want her left alone. Certainly not alone with Miss Evans. And at night, I want one of the staff to see her either to her room, or to his lordship's, and to check that the door is locked."

Thus was cast into motion Emma's returning to the manor. With that decision underway, before Dr. Wisely left the manor to visit other patients, he asked John Britely if he would please pick up Emma out at Wickenbird Farm and bring her to the manor. DCI Adams had reluctantly given his sanction.

"Of course," John Britely said. "I must say, I've thought that she should be here, but I recognized the danger for her. I'll call her now to make certain it's convenient for her to come as soon as I can get there." How to tell her without alarming her. Well, she had called him or Brooks every day to ask about his lordship. She wanted to be with him. She was already alarmed.

There had not been a more anxious drive than the one Emma took now with John Britely to Cav Neumont Manor, for this visit arose suddenly, and had Simon been improving, they would have waited until DCI Adams had solved the cause of her attack—her attacker. She would have known the result, and that the detective felt she was safe at the manor. As well, on the way John said that she was not to be left alone ever, and her door must be locked when she was in her room. She understood the real danger. As John Britely drove the Morgan around the circle, Hadley came down the stairs to greet Emma. "Ms. Chapman, we've so looked forward to your return, and we know, now that he has you near, that his lordship will recover." He couldn't bear to add his next thought, *he is deathly ill.*

Inside, Brooks greeted Emma and took her bag. She had merely brought her waist pack and a change of clothes. Under her jacket, she wore the new yellow percale dress that she had bought in the village. She wanted to appear as pretty as possible for Simon. Brooks took her jacket and waist pack. "I'll have these put in your usual room, Ms. Chapman. It's been reserved for you, of course. We've been worried about you, and so eager for your return. The doctor just arrived and is expecting you up in his lordship's room, and I'll bring a tray right on up for you."

"Brooks, so thoughtful as usual. I confess I am hungry, we rushed off so, and I've thought of nothing but being with his lordship again."

"I'm sure, Ms. Chapman. I'm sure it was hard being away from him, knowing he was so ill." Little did she know that his lordship was still in a coma, not responsive. Brooks felt pain for her. And for himself.

When Emma entered Simon's room, she saw the doctor and Pearce. Then she saw Simon, and he looked small, weak, and feverish. His face was sunken and sallow. Pearce was applying cold presses to Simon's brow. "I'd like to do that now if I may," she said.

"Of course, Ms. Chapman. He's waited so long for you." Pearce handed the cloth to Emma and pointed to the water basin nearby. Emma dipped the cloth in the cool water and rung it out, trying not to look at Simon. His tired, ill, face was almost too much for her to bear and her tears came, rolled, unhampered down her cheeks. Then, with one hand she pressed the cloth to his brow, and with her other hand she clasped his which lay by his side. She squeezed his hand. He did not respond. "I'm here, Simon. I'm here. I'm right here with you." She held on.

"A nurse will drop in later this afternoon to change his IV," Dr. Wisely said, "and I will check back in the morning about 9:00. Call me if there's any change." He said goodbye to Emma, and to Pearce who sat off to the side. Pearce had been instructed never to leave Emma alone; be certain before he left the room that either John Britely or Brooks, or Andy, or Peter, who had come down from college to help, took his place. Major kept watch right along with Pearce and Emma, or with whoever was there.

Emma had yet to get a response from Simon, but she continued to talk to him, continued to hold his hand, and continued to cool his brow. Sometimes Emma felt Simon shake and at those times she would lean over to enclose him in her arms, to hold him until he calmed. The tray of food that someone would bring up for her was often forgotten—allowed to become stale, and someone would come to replace it with a fresh tray.

Today, Brooks arrived with the tray. "Thank you kindly, Brooks," Emma said. "I just can't eat very much with my stomach in a knot so."

With Simon foremost on her mind, she hadn't reached DCI Adams yet to tell him that she now precisely remembered hiking Bingers with Brenda. She stepped through the small connecting study and into her room to phone the detective with this update. "Sir, I remember clearly the hike." She gave him the details. "However, I still have no idea what struck me. I remember bluebells and Brenda and then walking alone."

"We're almost there," he replied. "Not much of the puzzle is missing now, and it's an important piece of information that you do remember being with Miss Evans on the hike. Please be sure never to be left alone with his lordship. That is to say, one of the other men must stay with you."

At night, covered with a down throw that Ellie brought her, Emma caught a little sleep on the chesterfield not far from Simon's bed, a fitful sleep unable to go deep, always listening for Simon to call out. He had stopped calling for her. For the first two days that was how it went; Lord Haversham neither better nor worse. Throughout the manor there was not one smile, not one dry eye, not one happy feeling, not one light step save Brenda's. Not one soul could envision a life there without Lord Haversham. Someone, either Brooks or Hadley, would always take tea up to Emma and to whoever was on watch with her, and the others would have their regular tea in the drawing room—the mood not light-hearted though—no swapping of smart tales or clever aphorisms. Each one continued with his or her duties: cook supplying splendid dishes; John Britely keeping up with his lordship's business matters; Lady Mardling, Lady Southway and Sophia Bachman coming to call; Mrs. Penrose and Ellie organizing the household—keeping his lordship's bed linen fresh; Andy helping wherever he could; grounds men pruning; Hadley walking Bud, Maggie, and Major. But in all matters, there was no heart. Nothing was right without his lordship about.

During these days, Brenda knew that all that time, Emma was up in Simon's room; although she had not seen her, it was general knowledge—guarded hints spoken at tea. She asked to be let in to see Emma, and to help care for Simon. Excuses were invented right and left to deny her access to Simon's room. As DCI Adams had warned Brenda not to leave, and as no one at the manor would pay her attention, she decided to call Lady Claire. Her ladyship welcomed first-hand gossip about goings-on at the manor.

"They keep me out of Simon's room," Brenda complained. "I don't understand why. They went out of their way to bring Emma from the farm. I didn't see her come in, but I heard the whispers, and she's allowed in his room around the clock. I've never seen her leave it. She never comes down for tea. And apparently there is no restriction on anyone else being let into his room. I hear them speak of it."

"Well, you know, my dear, that from the start Ms. Chapman wormed her way into his attentions; definitely has him fooled. Potty thing! But that's no reason you shouldn't be allowed to visit him. I wonder just how ill he really is."

"Well, I've seen doctors and nurses coming and going daily, and I've heard talk about a doctor from London."

Then Lady Claire had a malicious idea. As Simon's former wife, she had lived at Cav Neumont Manor and knew its layout. "You know, dear, there is another way into Simon's room."

"There is?" Brenda's eyes widened up into a question.

"I know it well," Lady Claire said. "When I lived at the manor, my bedroom was Solar. And Solar connects to Simon's room through a small study."

"No." Brenda said. "I've been in Solar; it's the room Emma uses, and I haven't seen a connection to Simon's room."

"Indeed, there are two doors inside Solar. One leads into the dressing room and closets, and the other opens into a private study. And that study has a door into Simon's room. You can access Simon's room through Solar. There's also a hallway door into that study. If you look at the three hallway doors, moving northward, one is Solar, one is the study, and the next is Simon's. I should think one of those doors ought to work for you, and you have as much right into Simon's room as Ms. Chapman has." Naughty, naughty. It wasn't Lady Claire's business, but she would make it so. Help Brenda into Simon's room and gain access to more information. She didn't realize, however, what egregious act she was assisting.

Brenda was pumped with this news. Lady Claire knew everything, offered good advice. Certainly, there was no reason she shouldn't visit Simon. He must want her to; wondering why she hadn't done so. She resolved to give those doors a try. She had already found that Solar was kept locked, but she hadn't known about the study door; had thought it was a linen closet or such. With Ellie going in and out of Solar at times to clean, she, or perhaps even Emma, might forget to lock it. Now that she knew the connections to Simon's room, she would be vigilant about trying all doors. Eventually she would find one unlocked.

Meanwhile, DCI Adams had poked his nose into her medication issue. She knew she no longer needed those calming pills; doctors loved pushing pills. Whatever happened next, she needed to talk to Emma; find out whether Emma had any memory about what had happened on their hike. Thus she had two reasons to get into Simon's room: one, to see Simon, and the other to talk to Emma.

VII

At the Farm without Emma

Without Emma, Wickenbird Farm life and activities went on as usual: fires were built—smaller now—days were not quite as cold; Maida was served tea; Sara and Willa made tempting meals—adding exceptional flourishes as though something must be done to attempt to compensate for Emma's absence, if they could; Mars and Matt and Sol tended the outside needs—sheep, cows, orchards; Harvey and Jonquil, their cat, roamed or took their ease before the fire. But it was all different. Quite different. Subdued. Even at meals it was rare to hear laughter. No spontaneous repartee or jokes erupted as if Emma had carried away their humor. Each seemed to have one major thought: would Emma return to them? Or worse, would they even see her again? Emma had added a new bloom to the flowering of their days and now that bouquet had a vacant spot. Outside sensed the change as well: animals seemed quieter, not finding important reasons to neigh and bray. Though nothing had changed except for Emma's leaving, a pall had settled over the farm. However, she called once every day and Mars carried his phone about; that call the most important event of his daily life. Emma would tell him that she did so miss the farm and everyone there, but that his lordship had shown little improvement, his fever hanging on, and everyone at the manor was sad. And Mars would say that he was sorry to hear that, and though she was dearly missed at Wickenbird, everything else went on as expected. He couldn't reveal to her how deeply he personally missed her presence, and Emma couldn't tell him how deeply she regretted having to leave the farm. He would tell her that in the fall he would once again take a truck of produce and flowers to the market, and it would be excellent if she could join him: letting her know plans were in force. She would reply that she didn't know what the future months held for her. And so it went for a few days.

Then one day, while the waiting Earth stood still expectantly, Simon showed some response—not much, just a firm grasp of Emma's hand. She continued to read to him, and to that she had added some of his favorite music: Chopin's *Nocturnes*, Strauss' *Ein Heldenleben*. "Listen, Simon," she would say. "Listen to how long this oboist holds the note; I know you admire that solo." Possibilities were abundant—surely he could soon recover. She began to know that he would, and she told him that he was missed downstairs, before the fire, at tea and at table, and walking about. Bud wondered why he was not about, she said. Major expected him to get up. Schrödinger was despondent, always expecting him at meals. I need you to walk with me, she would continue. She would always tell Simon these things. She knew he heard her. His hand clasp grew firmer.

DCI Adams had not acted on Emma's new memories about the hike. It was still a situation of her word against Miss Evans'—who vowed she had never been on Bingers—and Emma's word that they had hiked Bingers; although she still had no idea what had happened to her there. DCI Adams much preferred to take Emma's word, but professionally he had to have more evidence. And even if they had been together on Bingers, that was not proof that Brenda had attacked Emma. And moreover, as an aside, he couldn't compel Brenda to take medication. Even if he spoke to her physician in the States, he had no authority in that regard.

After her phone call with Lady Claire, Brenda put her mind to gaining entry to Simon's room. The way she figured, she had as much right as anyone else. So she had begun to sit on a sturdy old settee that had stood perhaps for centuries at the end of her hallway, just inside the stained glass window, at the juncture of the hall to Simon's room. She always had a book, and would pretend to read, letting anyone who noticed her think that she loved that window and the lights it displayed. But her mind was not on the window or the book. Going down only for tea and meals, she was there to watch when someone entered or left Simon's room. She saw that Ellie sometimes went into Solar to clean, and occasionally a doctor or nurse, or one of the manor's residents, came and went. She herself appeared to be the only person denied access to the room. She would find her opportunity. One morning, rather than going down for breakfast, she decided to ask Ellie to bring a breakfast tray up to her room. It had occurred to her that maybe with all the morning commotion, people coming and going, more concerned about their appetites, she could find one of the three hall doors briefly left unlocked. And while no one was about, or at least it seemed so, she left her room and went down her hall to the settee where she waited a few minutes, and hearing nothing and seeing no one, she continued down Simon's hall trying first Emma's door—locked, and then the study door—unlocked. She slipped inside. She looked around the small study to assure that she was alone, and then waited to hear whatever she could. There was movement in the hallway, perhaps a breakfast tray being brought in. She selected a book and took a seat by the window. Should anyone come through, she would look seriously studious. Even Lady Joan would not be able to find fault. Brenda waited. With a door on one side of the study leading into Solar, and a door on the other side leading into Simon's room, Emma could be in either. After several such minutes listening, she tried the door into Simon's room. It gave way. She was pleased with this result, for it could have been locked from Simon's side, but she guessed that these days no one spent time in this small study, and no one was expected to be here. Even Pearce, Brenda reasoned, would have no reason to come into this small book-lined room. She waited a minute, then opened the door a larger space, enough to peer in. Simon's room was vast; she could see that from the small opening. She thought she could actually slip into the room and stand just inside his door without anyone knowing she was there. And she did just that, opening the door enough to slip through. The vast room was quiet as a tomb but no one could hear her on the Turkish carpet, and it was early enough that the drapery had not yet been drawn back. When her eyes had adjusted to the dim light, she saw Emma. Emma! Sitting by Simon's bed and drinking from a cup. And across to the side, shielded in a darkened corner, Brenda made out Andy. He was eating and looked surprised and watchful; he had seen her. She could see that Simon appeared to be sleeping peacefully. It was time to make herself known. Why ever not? Her efforts to win Simon's preference had taken a setback and it was time to remedy that.

"Hello, Emma. I've missed you," she said.

A shudder went through Emma as she jerked her head up at the shock of seeing someone enter through the study door, and especially seeing Brenda there. "Ah . . . hello, Brenda." Questions flooded in competing for Emma's speech, but she couldn't find the one to ask first. Then, finally as Brenda moved closer, Emma said, "I'm surprised to see you in Simon's study. I rather think none of us should be there."

"Well, all the other doors were locked and I really wanted to see Simon. I had heard you were back. I want to help."

Andy put down his fork and quit eating. Nothing bad was going to happen to Emma while he was there. He wasn't sure whether Brenda knew he was there, tucked in a corner as he was. He remained quiet, watching.

Brenda moved closer to Emma. This woman, she thought, this woman, Emma, had been a constant obstruction in her path to Simon, the block keeping her away from Simon's attentions. She could win him if Emma weren't about. She recalled how she had felt during their hike on Bingers—the field of bluebells. *Emma, why didn't you stay gone*? Then, almost without meaning to, she said it: "Emma, why didn't you stay gone?"

When Emma saw Brenda's expression, her suppressed memories rolled in like a sail unfurling, revealing everything that had happened. The truth lay on Brenda's face—her stiffened, rigid lips thinned into a firm line; face pulled into tight eyes. Now Emma knew exactly what had attacked her and she felt anew the terror for Brenda's striking her as they had turned on Bingers to thread their way back. She could precisely remember the moment before the attack, and waking later in the bluebells. Alone. Brenda had struck her—probably with her hiking stick.

"Yes, it was I who hit you, Emma. I struck you over and over." Brenda, with aroused and uncontrolled anger, ignored Andy's presence in the corner. "I tried to kill you. You were in my way. You are still in my way. Why didn't you stay where you were?" She moved closer, reached around Emma, and from an end table by Simon's bed, she picked up a small bronze lion. She couldn't help herself; whatever else happened, Emma had to go. As she reached, she purposely upended Emma's cup, then raised the lion at the very instant that Andy leapt across the room, knocking over his breakfast tray. In the great noise and commotion, it seemed not at all out of line for a tornado to sweep into the room, thrashing everything about. Lady Joan stared at Brenda. The tornado increased and within it, Lady Joan circled Brenda, electricity jolted the air, not letting up, not releasing Brenda until she screamed and yelled; confessed to Simon, who now, if their eyes could believe, was sitting up in bed, looking for all the world very much alive and well.

"Simon, I tried to remove Emma from the manor, from your life," Brenda yelled. "I'm better for you than she is. I need a chance with you. Without her around you would see that in time. Time is all I need."

By now, Andy had grabbed Brenda. Emma reached to the rope by Simon's bed, giving it great frantic jerks to summon help. The tornado died down and Lady Joan, casting her reassuring glance over all, slowly drifted off. And, as was her custom, she didn't bother taking a door, just went straight through a wall. Emma stood on the spilt food to hug Simon. "Simon . . . dear Simon. Thank God! I've been so worried." She clung to him. Simon's eyes were opened wide to see her, and he tried his voice. "I'm back Emma. I've been in a long dark place, but I knew you were here, and that I had to come back."

Brooks, flying into the room, stopped suddenly to survey the situation: dishes all over, food spread about on the floor, and Andy struggling with Brenda. Without being told, Brooks knew what had happened. He rang for Ellie and Pearce to come help with the clean-up, then he and Andy dragged Brenda—who was yelling to Simon, that he would see, in time he would see that she was right—out of the way and down the hall to her own room. They waited with her while putting in a call to DCI Adams.

The detectives sped to the manor. They had spoken to Andy and had heard that Brenda confessed to trying to kill Emma, and had tried again to attack her. While Brooks and Andy waited for the detectives to arrive, they sat with Brenda until she became subdued and even contrite. She looked to be in shock, not sure of what was going on, but she sat quietly. When the detectives arrived, Hadley showed them straight up to Brenda's room. She submitted to being handcuffed— necessary because they now knew she was capable of violence, and with those restraints in place, the men began to relax. DCI Adams asked that Emma be sent for. He needed to hear from her, as well as Andy, what had happened. They waited silently until Emma came into the room, and then DCI Adams started his questioning. First, he asked Andy exactly what had happened. Andy related the same information that he had given him over the phone. Then DCI Adams asked Emma what she had experienced.

"I was sitting by Simon's bedside, and Andy was sitting across the room, when I heard something and looked to see Brenda coming into the room from the side study. That surprised me . . . that she did not come in from the hallway. She said hello, to which I replied." Emma related as much of what had transpired, as much as she could remember—it had all happened so fast. "She said she wanted to see Simon, and that she had tried to kill me, and why didn't I stay gone. She said pretty much the same to Simon who seems to have been awakened from his coma by the terror. So I think he might be a witness to what she said. And when I saw the frightening look on her face, I had total recall of being bludgeoned by her, for she had that same look before we turned to start the hike back. I remember being puzzled by that look, evil, I thought." Still, in all of this, Emma felt for Brenda. Wished she did not have to utter such incriminating remarks. "And then in a moment, before I could react, she had a little statue raised to strike me with it. Then such a commotion with Brenda telling Simon, who was sitting up, how she had tried to get rid of me." Emma stopped speaking and looked at Brenda. "I'm so sorry for you, Brenda." Emma went on to describe what she thought happened next. "Thank God Andy was there. He grabbed Brenda and restrained her, while I pulled the rope for help." She didn't think it would be wise to mention Lady Joan's role; the detective might not understand the manor's ghost. And Emma did need to appear to be a reliable witness.

Then DS Adams turned to Brenda. "Miss Evans, you do not have to say anything. But it may harm your defense if you do not mention, when questioned, something which you later rely on in court. Anything you do say may be given in evidence. Do you understand me?" Under British law, he had to read her her rights, but considering her illness, as he understood it, she would probably be sent, accompanied somehow, right back to the States. Now though, it was critical to get her out of the manor and into a hospital, and under the right medication so she couldn't hurt anyone. Brenda remained resolute, yielding reluctantly a slight nod.

"Please tell us, Miss Evans, exactly what you did, and what you meant to do." Both he and DS Sanders had notebooks and pens in hand.

"I don't know," she said. "I didn't mean to do anything. This is all a mistake."

"But, Miss Evans, both Ms. Chapman and Mr. Sullivan caught you in the act of picking up a sculpture and raising it to strike Ms. Chapman. And they say that you confessed to trying to kill her. How do you explain that?"

"Andy was dreaming. He was asleep, couldn't have heard anything. I merely wanted to speak to my good friend, Emma, who has been away. And I wanted to help with Simon. Emma doesn't want me to help with Simon, and she has made up a story to explain why she was trying to chase me out. She threw her coffee at me!" Then she remembered the statue. "I picked up the lion because it was about to be knocked over."

Andy shook his head *no*. DCI Adams could see that he would get nowhere with this woman, would not be able to get at the truth, and now that he had witnesses to her violence, he had to take her in. "You must come with us, Miss Evans." She offered no resistance as the detectives pulled her up out of the chair and led her downstairs to a patrol car.

After he had delivered her to the clinic, where she would be locked in a room and cared for until they figured out what to do next, DCI Adams phoned Luke Williams and told him what had happened. Luke was the only person the detective knew, who had an interest in Miss Evans' welfare. Luke said he would be over as soon as he could get a ticket. He would bring her home. If she were on the medication, she probably, by that time, would not be a threat.

VIII

Simon's Progress

With Emma on his arm, Simon began to walk about his room. They took their meals there where Brooks would lay the table for them in the window through which they could watch spring advancing, see the lilacs begin their annual display. With breakfast, Brooks would bring in the paper, and after Emma and Simon had exhausted the wonder they felt, and any news circling about, they would read together. Soon, Simon was strong enough to go down. He wanted to see something different, wanted to say hello to all his staff. They each, he knew, had done everything he and she could on his behalf. And after two mornings sitting in his room, eating there with Emma, reading with Emma, walking down the hall with Emma to examine the light playing through the brilliant window, Pearce helped him dress, and he and Emma surprised everyone by appearing in the morning room for breakfast. Schrödinger was waiting on his perch. How could he have known that Simon was coming down, everyone wondered. But he had known. And Simon took additional bacon and sausage just to have extra morsels to celebrate with Schrödinger.

Simon wanted to walk throughout the manor. He asked everyone, when they had finished eating to take that walk with him, let him sense the manor's wonderful rooms and places through the eyes and souls of each. Major should come as well, he said. And so, at the agreed moment, when all had finished with breakfast, the great tour began. Brooks and Emma were worried about Simon's strength for such a tour, but he was recovering by the second; happiness was his medication, hope his recuperation. Schrödinger was not to be left behind; this event was too rare, too significant, a cat must be on call to witness it, and he trailed along. He also loved the manor's rooms.

By now, all was revealed about the fateful hike. Before Brenda could strike Emma with the lion, her eyes and mouth had tightened into hatred, and had brought back to Emma the moment she had seen that face on Brenda when they had turned around to hike back out of the bluebells. She realized Brenda had struck her then. After Emma told DCI Adams that she and Brenda had left the manor by way of the south terrace, and in that hallway entrance had picked up hiking sticks before leaving, and that she vividly remembered the hike now, and the look of rage on Brenda's face—DCI Adams had DS Sanders gather the sticks from that hallway, and have them examined for traces of a crime. It was then that spots of blood, proven to be Emma's, were found on one of the heaviest sticks.

Luke came for Brenda. She was declared to be ill, but safe to return home with Luke as long as she continued on medication; Luke would see to that. By the time she was ready to leave the clinic, she was calm, accepting that she really needed to go home, really needed to return to work. Luke had missed her greatly he said, and she remembered how important he had been in her life. She had already, it appeared, forgotten about Simon and the manor.

With her gone from the manor now, and Simon almost back to his old self, Emma often on his arm or holding his hand, her telling him again and again her prayers had been answered, and his feeling that he had received one more gift from the universe—the manor was once more its jolly self with friends stopping by: Sophia Bachman and Lady Mardling and Lady Southway. Andy had stayed on a while also. Simon had urged him to use the manor as a base for his archaeological studies for as long as he could, for they enjoyed his company. So all in all, there were many people to dine with them, and around the table once more, light-hearted repartee and swapping of stories took place. Schrödinger on his perch as well felt that the universe had handed him a blessing: Simon was back. Major sat at Simon's feet. Emma sat at his right. Lady Mardling and Lady Southway, less acerbic now, competed for the place at his left, but more gracefully than in the past, in consideration for his lordship's fragile health. The bouquet continued to be kept fresh at the table's foot. Brooks and Hadley and cook were spritelier than ever, happy in the knowledge that all was once again on course.

Something new had been added though: frequent visits back and forth from the manor to Wickenbird Farm. The Marsdens, along with Sara, Jane, Sol and Matt, were invited to visit and dine at the manor. Even Maida was brought along on one occasion. So now, at many of those meals, there were Lord Haversham, Emma, John Britely, Andy, Sophia, Mars, Hannah, Sol, and Matt, and both of the esteemed and titled ladies. Jane stayed home because of school demands; Josh and Peter were away at college. At other times when she was not at work, Emma, Lord Haversham, John Britely, and Andy would spend a few days at Wickenbird Farm. On occasion they would bring Sophia with them. The two groups of very well-meaning people became close friends, and now his lordship's circle of company and friends was great indeed. No longer was his life as lonely as previously.

As for Lady Claire, her bridges were burnt too thoroughly with Brenda gone, so that now she had to be content with infrequent titbits of gossip that Lady Mardling could pass along. And in time, when she picked up her chairs at Wickenbird Farm it wouldn't be Emma and Mars whom she found in holy matrimony, but perhaps Hannah and Andy—perhaps not in holy matrimony, but looking very close.

IX

In the Right Amount of Time

In the right amount of time: that most perfect time and perfect day, Emma Chapman and Lord Simon Appleby Haversham, 5th Earl of Cav Neumont, were married. The wedding took place in the chapel at Cav Neumont Manor with all their friends, relatives, staff, and pets present. Peter served as best man and Josh gave his mother away. Hannah made the perfect bridesmaid. And though Emma and Simon had insisted on keeping the wedding simple, Mrs. Penrose, Brooks, cook and all their helpers had scurried about finding new ways to dress up the manor, and to prepare a feast to top all other feasts. Sara had come in from the farm to assist with the festivities. And the wedding attendees were already thinking about food and champagne. One could have been forgiven for thinking that Emma and Simon were in the first blush of romance as they savored their joy, their eyes caressing each other in wonderment. When their vows came to conclusion, followed by the kiss all had waited for, and Emma turned to show her affection for all the guests: there was Mars holding Sophia's hand; Andy had taken Hannah's; Sol was holding Sara's; Greg and Mary Tortle were as usual hand in hand; John Britely's romance was blooming and he had warned Simon that he might bring an addition to the manor soon, and there he stood with her, holding hands. It was almost as though there wasn't an uncoupled hand in the room. The manor seemed to Emma to breed love and coupling. Through her own tears she could see Aunt Ola's tears topping a smile that bespoke her happiness. And there, off in a corner, standing in respectful silence, Major and Schrödinger. Even Lady Joan, in another corner unseen by most—if Emma could believe it—shed a ghost tear. Lady Mardling's and Lady Southway's hands went unheld. Even so, they looked content and appeared to know that time would sense that omission and work its magic. Lord Haversham seemed to invent opportunities to refer to Emma as Lady Haversham. Everything works out in the strength of time.